The Alexandria Scrolls

GORDON DONNELL

iUniverse, Inc.
New York   Bloomington

iUniverse books may be ordered through booksellers or by contacting:

iUniverse
1663 Liberty Drive
Bloomington, IN 47403
www.iuniverse.com
1-800-Authors (1-800-288-4677)

Because of the dynamic nature of the Internet, any Web addresses or links contained in this book may have changed since publication and may no longer be valid. The views expressed in this work are solely those of the author and do not necessarily reflect the views of the publisher, and the publisher hereby disclaims any responsibility for them.

ISBN: 978-1-4502-1426-1 (sc)
ISBN: 978-1-4502-1427-8 (ebook)

Printed in the United States of America

iUniverse rev. date: 02/25/2010

Chapter 1

The monastery loomed up out of the mist, built slightly off-kilter to follow the contours of a commanding escarpment. Stone walls topped by medieval battlements and over-shadowed by a partially ruined tower made me think of Castle Dracula.

"It was in mountain sanctuaries such as this," Eddington lectured, "that the Georgian Orthodox church held out against centuries of Muslim invasion."

Eddington's girth monopolized the back seat of the Land Cruiser as effectively as his Oxford wheeze monopolized conversation. Broad knowledge suggested substantial reading during his fifty-odd years, though not all of it at British Universities. The tobacco in his Meerschaum was a near-eastern blend that turned the Toyota into a gas chamber. I opened the front passenger window and let in the icy drizzle.

"The Muslim threat seems to have receded," I remarked.

Gregoriev let out a humorless laugh from the driver's seat. "We are twelve kilometers only from Chechen border."

Gregoriev was our translator and Eddington's choice to supervise the dig. He had a wrestler's bulk and he needed it to keep the Land Cruiser on the rugged access road.

The track ended at a ravine. The monastery walls rose straight up from the far side without so much as a toehold between them and the vertical granite beneath. Spanning the intervening chasm was a stone bridge that crossed to a pair of oak doors.

Eddington knocked the ash out of his pipe.

"Gregoriev and I will go in," he informed me. "You will remain with the vehicle."

"I'll come with you," I said.

Today Georgia was just another down-at-the-heels former Soviet Republic but once it had been the fabled land of Colchis. Everyone from the Argonauts to Ghengis Khan had passed through. If there were secrets to be seen, I was determined to get a look.

"I shouldn't have to remind you," Eddington said, "that I am in charge here."

"Unless the Falkenberg Foundation writes a check," I reminded him, "there won't be anything to be in charge of."

Once upon a time Alex Falkenberg and I had worked for the same high-tech start-up. Stock options and starvation salaries. When the company was bought out, bean counters like me walked away with enough money that we wouldn't have to work for a while. Falkenberg had been a vice president. He walked away set for life.   The only thing we shared was a fascination with history. He set up a foundation to fund archaeological digs. The foundation paid my expenses to assess feasibility. It sounded proper and professional. In reality we were two amateurs with a bloated bankroll. That was a recipe for trouble and when one of the oak doors opened, I wondered how much I'd stepped into.

The monk who strode across the bridge was seven feet tall. Gaunt to the point of cadaverous, he had flowing hair and eyes that penetrated the depths of mortal souls. His English was good enough to let Eddington know who was really in charge. He patted us for concealed weapons, went through my backpack for explosives and then led the way across the bridge. I brought up the rear.

Drizzle had left the stone surface slick. Mist beneath made the ravine look bottomless and hungry. Beyond the oak door lay a claustrophobic stone passageway. We went under the iron spikes of a raised portcullis and into another world.

An artist's hand was evident in the monastery's design; artisanship in its construction. Surrounding a central courtyard was a colonnade floored in intricate mosaic, with rococo arches supporting walls pierced by lancet windows. It was immaculate and empty, save for a work party of monks on their hands and knees scrubbing. A pristine slice of time and culture, fortified against the siege of progress.

The monk who emerged from a door at the base of the tower was beyond discernible age. His pace was measured, his countenance serene. He greeted Eddington and Gregoriev. I spoke no Georgian and didn't get even the gist of what passed between them.

The old gentleman led Eddington and Gregoriev into the tower. I wasn't invited.

My seven foot escort considered me with his scary eyes. "You are English?"

"American."

I probably didn't look it. Except for long underwear and steel-toed boots, the clothes I brought from Seattle weren't up to a trip into the Caucasus Mountains. I had found a great coat and a Soviet Army ushanka in a surplus store in Tblisi. I handed Friar Bones one of my Foundation business cards.

"Owen Doran." He pronounced my name gravely, as if I shouldn't expect too much when Judgment Day arrived. "You have not come seeking God."

I wasn't entirely sure why we had come. This was a detour on the way to a proposed dig site the Foundation had sent me to evaluate. The monks had something and Eddington was hot to look at it.

"Do you happen to have these Alexandria Scrolls on CD?" I asked.

The question was just to test his reaction. I didn't expect him to quote a price. Particularly not as steep as the one he came up with. Once my book-keeper's rebellion subsided I started thinking. Eddington was no fool. And the aging splendor around me raised the possibility that something significant might lie hidden here. The money was Falkenberg's so I agreed.

Friar Bones summoned a monk from the work party and gave instructions. "You know your traveling companions well?" he asked when the fellow had scampered off.

"I met them two days ago." A call from Falkenberg had sent me scrambling to Tblisi with instructions to contact a Professor Eddington.

"They carry the stink of Hell."

Friar Bones was no fragrant petunia himself but I kept my mouth shut.

"You must keep your wits upon you," he warned.

"You make it sound like I should have brought a .45."

I was kidding.

He wasn't.

He crooked a finger for me to follow, led the way along the colonnade and unlocked a heavy door. Fluorescent ceiling tubes sputtered and sizzled and lit up a storeroom. Stencils on the nearest crates were Cyrillic.

My Russian was none too spiffy but I knew what *Automat Kalashnikov* meant.

The handgun inventory didn't include any actual .45s. All were foreign automatics. I recognized only a Luger, probably left over from the Nazi occupation. Like a lot of nerds who grew up on bad movies and worse television, I had always wanted my own Luger.

Friar Bones knew a sucker when he saw one. He was firm on price but he offered to throw in a box of nine millimeter hardball and two soles of hash. I told him I didn't smoke dope. He warned me it wasn't wise to travel in the mountains without trade goods. The monastery's satellite uplink made short work of the Falkenberg Foundation's credit card. Friar Bones and I were back out in the courtyard when Eddington and Gregoriev reappeared.

"Did you get what you wanted?" I asked when the three of us were in the Toyota and moving again.

"That does not concern the Foundation," Eddington informed me.

It would as soon as I got a look at the contents of the CD I'd stuffed into my backpack with the rest of my loot. I digested my impression of the monastery while I cleaned the drizzle off my glasses.

The monks weren't the western stereotype of pious characters stomping grapes and chanting hymns but drug trafficking and gun running fit what I had heard of the local context. A toke of hash was regarded the same way Americans looked at a stiff drink after work. And law enforcement was spotty enough to make firearms a household necessity. Although I did wonder about the crates of thirty seven millimeter anti-aircraft ammunition I'd seen in the holy weapons bazaar.

We reached the paved road that wound through the mountain pass. Aside from Gregoriev's remark about the Chechen border and a GPS reading that I'd taken at the monastery, I had no idea where we were. Archaeologists were notoriously tight-lipped about dig sites. Looting was an international industry. There was a lucrative black market in antiquities.

A couple of kilometers of forest went by and then Gregoriev turned off and I learned why we had spare tires lashed to the roof of the Land Cruiser. The track we followed was older than sin and a lot rougher. Sharp stones accounted for the right rear in ten minutes. The drizzle turned to rain when we got out to make the change.

The vegetation thinned as we climbed. A few hundred feet below snow level we reached a camp. A peasant guard with an AK-47 slung muzzle-down glanced in at Gregoriev and passed us. An hour of daylight remained for me to look over the site. There were several guards and they seemed amused by my meanderings. I wasn't robustly built and with the ear flaps of my ushanka down and the collar of my great coat up I probably looked like a wandering tent.

Excavation had been started and abandoned, not recently. Exposed fragments of ancient stone floors and broken walls offered no hint of who would settle in this godforsaken spot. Or why.

"What am I looking at here?" I asked Eddington. "I mean, what does all this represent?"

"In the broadest sense," he said, "you may be witness to the factual soundness of major religious scripture, albeit writing plagiarized from earlier lore."

"Can you be a little more specific?"

"What would be the point? You are here to assess feasibility. There has been excavation, ergo excavation is feasible."

"The excavation was abandoned. Maybe they found it wasn't feasible."

"It was abandoned," Eddington said, "when the Soviet Union fell and money for cultural pursuits ran out."

Apparently the lectures were over. He clumped off to continue his own inspection. I went over to the fire to see what was cooking.

Dinner was thin soup and dark bread. The trick was to soak the bread in the soup until it was soft enough that you could bite into it without breaking a tooth. Taste-wise it was a notch below even the chowder and sandwich lunches I'd survived on in the high tech industry.

That night I had a two-man tent to myself. It was cold and drafty but there was only one leak of any significance. I typed a few notes on my laptop and then slipped Friar Bones' CD into the drive to be sure he hadn't stiffed me with *The Greatest Hits of Garnet Mims and the Enchanters*.

What I saw chilled my blood. Scan after scan of densely packed script. The writing looked to be very old Greek. It had that cramped, linear perfection that ancient scribes spent their lives mastering. The last time I'd seen anything comparable was on fragments displayed during a tour of the *Dead Sea Scrolls*. My hands were shaking when I opened my backpack to put it away.

I was in a lawless land, among people I didn't know, in possession of something potentially priceless. My eyes fell on the Luger. The limit of my weapons experience was shooting Grandpa Doran's bolt action .22 rifle when I was a kid but even the illusion of security was a comfort. I loaded the magazine and chambered a round.

The rain had picked up. There was a small river running through the tent. I stowed everything in the backpack and used it for a pillow on the canvas cot. I lay fully dressed, boots and all, under a rough woolen blanket, trying to keep warm enough to sleep. Sometime in the night I heard the rain turn to wind-driven sleet.

Then I heard the noises.

They were soft and very close outside the tent and I was wide awake and full of dread. I rolled quietly to a sitting position on the cot, put on my glasses and slipped my hand inside the back-pack where I had stashed the Luger.

A three round burst of automatic gunfire nearly tore out my eardrums. The flashes lanced through the tent wall. I felt bullets hammer into the taut canvas where I had lain. The tent flap opened. A face appeared. It was a demon face, indistinct and red in the faint glow of the still-burning camp fire. Reflex brought up the Luger. I felt it buck in my hand.

The face disappeared in the muzzle flash. I charged out of the tent under a full head of adrenaline, swinging my back pack. The pack connected with something solid. A rifle discharged. I triggered two panic-stricken shots into a dark figure and took off running.

Behind me the camp exploded in gunfire. Terror carried me down the slope past the Land Cruiser, picking me up when I fell, suppressing the pain when I barked my shins, driving me relentlessly. I ran until my legs were rubber and my lungs were on fire and then sat down gasping and tried to hear through the ringing in my ears.

The night had fallen silent. I had no clue what had happened. I wondered what had become of Eddington. I thought briefly about sneaking back for a look but I was spent and shivering and scared shitless.

Not that chickening out would be a whole lot easier. That involved finding my way down a mountain track in the dark, making my way back to civilization in a country I didn't know and raising help from people whose language I didn't speak.

Chapter 2

Alex Falkenberg kept a penthouse condominium in San Francisco. I hadn't been summoned recently and he had changed lady friends in my absence. The woman who answered the chimes stood tall enough to look me in the eyes. Black hair fell straight and curled inward, framing the alabaster symmetry of her face. A midnight blue cocktail sheath showed no skin whatever. It didn't need to.

"I am Sofia." She pronounced it So-Fie-Yah in a softly accented contralto that left me mumbling my introduction.

I fumbled my dripping umbrella into an antique stand full of dripping umbrellas. She found room for my coat in a closet crowded with pricier outerwear. Convivial chatter filtered through pocket doors that closed off the parlor. She led me the other way, along a hall.

Her fragrance was the kind I could feel as much as smell. I caught myself wondering whether her headlights were original equipment. Not that it mattered. Only Falkenberg could afford the ride. She opened the door to his study and closed it behind me.

Alexander the Great was in fine form, pacing the Persian carpet in a dinner jacket and talking a mile a minute into a Bluetooth, punctuating the conversation with gestures at walls of bookshelves. A peal of thunder drowned his words and rain clawed at the windows, reducing the night-lit city to a blur. He saw me, snapped, "Later," and threw the Bluetooth onto a teak desk.

"About time," he all but yelled. "I send you to do a simple job and you lose a Professor of Classical History to Chechen bandits and then vanish for a week yourself."

I set my zipper case on the corner of the desk and went to the sideboard. "Glad to see you're well, Owen, old chum," I said. "Heard about your encounter in the mountains. Nasty business, that. Here, let me make you a drink. Cuba Libre, wasn't it?"

We were polar opposites, Falkenberg and I. Visually we were older versions of the wimp and the blimp from junior high school. In real terms Falkenberg was a player. He never lost sight of the big picture and he could go from bulldozer aggressiveness to fawning charm to pull it together. I had never seen his courage or his confidence falter. If he didn't need cheap help to mind the details for him, I would still be Walter Mitty, concocting grand adventures in my imagination. He moved close enough to make his bulk obvious and intimidating.

"Well?" he demanded.

"Any job looks simple if you stand far enough away from it," I said.

He subsided into one of the room's Victorian wing chairs. "Just tell me what happened."

I settled into the other and told him about my escape from the dig site, omitting the shooting I had done. It was dawn when I reached the pass and flagged down a truck. The driver spoke no English. All I could do was wave the two soles of hash in his face and keep repeating, "Tblisi, Tblisi," until he nodded agreement.

I also didn't mention my stop at the international express office where I bubble-wrapped my laptop, GPS and digital camera into an approximate rectangle to hide the Luger from intruding X-ray machines.

The Embassy was surprised to see me. I had already been reported killed. Two guards had also escaped. They had seen Eddington hauled off by Chechen bandits. The Embassy had recovered my luggage from the hotel so it was no chore to clean me up and get me to the police to put in my two cents. I kept it simple. It was night. I was scared. I ran for my life. I saw nothing.

I didn't know whether the investigator believed me or just had too much work piled up to waste time on dumb-ass foreigners. The Embassy impressed on me the importance of emerging U.S. relations with the Georgian Republic, strongly suggested that I not discuss my experience with anyone and hustled me onto the first Ilyushin heading west. I made Istanbul to London to Seattle on my own, glad to get back on American soil.

"So," Falkenberg said, getting up to make one of his trademark champagne cocktails, "you went home, put your feet up for a week and didn't answer the phone."

"I went home," I said, joining him at the sideboard to mix myself a refill, "to work on your feasibility assessment."

That was true only in the factual sense. I had once read that the great initial shock of combat was the realization that someone wanted to kill you. I had no concept of how powerful or persistent that shock could be. I had spent the week drinking too much, not sleeping well and trying to recover a semblance of equilibrium.

Falkenberg gave me the skeptical snort I deserved. "Let's see what you came up with."

The packet was skimpy. Snapshots of the dig site and GPS coordinates that put it close to Pankisi Gorge, which several websites listed as a Chechen rebel stronghold.

"You'll find a fat credit card charge in the expenses," I said. "This is what it bought."

He scowled, first at the CD I had received from Friar Bones and then at me. "What is it?"

"The Alexandria Scrolls," I said, curious to see what his reaction would be.

"How sure are you?"

The question was vehement enough to startle me. His eyes burned hot and impatient for an answer. I told him about Eddington's side trip to the monastery.

Falkenberg took the CD delicately between his fingertips. "I want your assurance this is the only copy."

I sat down and made a face at him over my glass. "Okay, Alex. Spit it out."

"What?"

"You sent me into a godforsaken corner of the world, nearly got me killed and now you're treating a CD like Ming china and you want an exclusive on material you haven't even seen. What's this about?"

He paraded to the wall and swung out a framed oil. The safe-behind-the-painting routine was as trite as it got but Falkenberg had a thing for the trappings of old money.

"How would you," he asked while he twirled the dial, "like to strip away the religious drivel from the *Book of Exodus* and put it in its rightful place as history?"

The question came out of the blue and left me staring. "They're liable to revoke your bar mitzvah," I warned.

He locked the CD away and swung the painting back into place. "Don't be facetious."

"Okay," I allowed. "The least I can do in common politeness is listen to you explain how one CD can discredit religious writing that has lasted through twenty five hundred years of conquest and repression."

Just translating the contents would be daunting. The CD was packed with scans. Each would have to be laid out in a grid and gone over word by word. Teams of experts would be required.

Falkenberg retrieved his champagne cocktail and sat down. He contemplated the liquid before he allowed himself a sip.

"Reach back into your uptight Presbyterian upbringing," he instructed, "and tell me what you remember about the Exodus."

I hadn't been to church in years and I doubted Falkenberg had either. "The Hebrews were slaves in Egypt. Moses said let my people go. The Pharaoh said forget it. God sent down ten plagues and drowned the Egyptian army. The Hebrews got out of Dodge, conquered Canaan and settled down to the usual sex and violence."

Falkenberg came to his feet and began pacing. "You've heard of the Santorini eruption?"

"Mediterranean island volcano," I recalled. "Blew itself to smithereens around 1600 BC. Possibly the source of the legend of the lost continent of Atlantis."

"But certainly," Falkenberg said, "an integral part of the natural phenomena described in *Exodus* as the ten plagues of Egypt." He stopped pacing, added, "Natural, not divine, phenomena," and took a belt from his champagne cocktail to emphasize the point.

Never one to object to a drink, I joined him. "How," I inquired, suitably fortified, "does a Greek island blow up and fill Egypt full of frogs and locusts?"

"The Santorini eruption," he went on, stalking the confines of the room again and seeming to draw energy from the violent weather outside, "was not an isolated incident. Underlying the eastern Mediterranean is a vast geological fault system. The eruption was only one of a series of venting activities along the system. Release of subterranean gasses poisoned the Nile, driving out frogs and flies, thereby unleashing pestilence. The eruption itself caused the rain of fire and ice, natural fallout from any volcanic storm. The ash cloud blotted out the sun and reduced temperatures, a biological signal for hordes of locusts to land."

"What about the other mischief?" I asked. "Wasn't there something about the first born male child of every Egyptian household dying?"

"A release of carbon dioxide, which is heavier than air, would have suffocated anyone sleeping on low furniture, which, in Egypt, was a favored position conferred upon first born males. Ten plagues, one natural sequence of events, no God required."

It was an effort to keep from rolling my eyes. "Aren't you blowing a Sunday school fairy tale out of proportion? I mean, the only place the story crops up is in *Exodus*. You'd think the Egyptians would have noticed something. Maybe mentioned it in their own writings."

Falkenberg stopped and towered over me, beaming with superior knowledge. "Recently a stela from the reign of Pharaoh Akmose was rediscovered in the Cairo museum. It described in detail many of the same natural disasters recorded in *Exodus*. Akmose's reign was contemporaneous with the Santorini eruption. His first born son died at the age of twelve. And he presided over an event known in Egyptian history as the Hyksos expulsion, which the Egyptians saw as cleansing the land of foreigners."

Falkenberg was wound tighter than I had seen him in a long time. I recalled that Eddington had mentioned scripture in connection with the dig site.

"What exactly do these Alexandria Scrolls have to do with re-writing the Bible?" I asked.

"If they don't contain direct evidence," Falkenberg said, moving again, "they may provide clues to other sources that will elevate the facts of *Exodus* into legitimate history and flush the religion into the sewer of superstition where it belongs."

Lightning illuminated the room like the flash of a strobe. The boom of thunder came no more than a two count behind and shook the window glass. I imagined old Mose throwing the power of God around the heavens while the molecule men closed in on him. Since I had obviously already had too much to drink I didn't see any harm in getting up to mix myself another.

"How much did Eddington tell you about the Scrolls?" Falkenberg asked.

Fessing up that Eddington hadn't told me squat would only persuade Falkenberg to clam up too. In his view, candor was a one way virtue. I needed to piss him off to keep him babbling.

"I hope you two fruit loops aren't looking for an hour of fame on *The History Channel*. The entire population of the Bible belt is liable to show up on your doorstep and burn you at the stake for living in sin with So-Fie-Yah."

"I'm serious," he insisted.

"So am I. I didn't say anything about the last one. What was her name? Barbara? She looked like a social climber with a two bounce a week limit. But this new honey is the real deal. If you've got a scrap of common sense, you'll take advantage of your next bout of post-coital depression to dump her."

He just smiled. "Wrong. About both women."

Samson and Delilah came to mind, although in Falkenberg's case nature hadn't left much for the scissors. "Well, it's your neck. Speaking of necks, is there any word on Eddington?"

"I was just on the phone with that department head at his college. They don't know shit and I--"

The door opened and Sofia stepped in. "Alexander, you have guests."

"Sorry," I said, finishing my drink and putting the glass aside. "I didn't mean to barge in. You should have told me it was party night."

Sofia delivered Falkenberg to the parlor and helped me with my coat. She took my free hand in both of hers.

"You will help Alexander?"

Warm eyes made the question a plea. That level of attention from a trophy class chick was enough to set my head spinning. Downing three highballs in twenty minutes gave me enough nerve to peck her on the cheek but not enough to try for a juicier target. I probably read too much into the fact that she didn't recoil.

Riding down alone in the elevator gave me time to stew over a couple of things that had bothered me all week.

First was my escape from the mountains. I was no believer in coincidence, unless it worked against me. The fact that I had a gun with me when I needed it and two soles of hash when I needed them meant Friar Bones had at least some inkling of what was going to happen, although I couldn't fathom why he would help a heathen stranger.

Second was the bandit attack. If you're a kidnapper, you need someone to carry the ransom note. I was the perfect candidate. I was western, I was a witness and the raiders could scare the crap out of me without half trying. Yet they had opened their attack with an attempt on my life.

And now there was Falkenberg and the Scrolls. I didn't object to a little recreational Bible bashing. I still resented the years I had spent in Sunday school acquiring the skills I would use later in life to strike out with good girls who were looking for bad boys. But Falkenberg was serious and so was Eddington. That raised the possibility that I had stumbled onto something important. If I hadn't had three shots of eighty proof courage, the idea probably would have panicked me. Instead I started mulling over ways to learn more.

Chapter 3

San Sebastian College was a private institution where well-heeled parents could warehouse their under-achieving offspring with no fear of exposing them to political incorrectness. Tyrone Berryman was the ideal department head; a trim African American who rhapsodized about taking academic endeavor to the next level.

"Recruiting an Oxford graduate of Professor Eddington's caliber," he told me while we waited on a flagstone path for the arc of a sprinkler to pass, "was the first step in upgrading to a premier faculty."

Berryman had suggested we walk while we talked, since it was such a nice day. My guess was that hiring Eddington had upped the threat level for the laid back wine-and-cheese crowd who normally haunted small college faculty rosters and he was afraid the hallowed halls had ears.

"Eddington was quite a catch," I agreed. "I'm surprised you let him trek off into the Caucasus Mountains?"

"An educator immersed in research can provide his students a far more relevant learning experience."

Little cliques of students were sunning themselves on acres of professionally tended lawn. I doubted that much of what they were learning came from anyone over twenty. Rummaging in the pockets of my tweed sport coat made me feel like a fossil. I handed Berryman a page I had printed from Friar Bones' CD.

Judging from his indulgent smile he unfolded it out of politeness rather than curiosity. It took only a glance at the contents to adjust his attitude. He fumbled inside his suit coat and found a pair of bifocals. He scanned the densely packed old writing and his administrator's veneer peeled away.

"Where did you get this?" His chestnut eyes searched my face, full of suspicion.

"Grant me access to a folder on your FTP site," I said. "I'll deliver the Alexandria Scrolls in soft copy within two days."

A lottery winner's disbelief flickered through his suspicion. He folded the sheet and tucked it into his pocket, the quick movement of a squirrel stashing a purloined acorn before it could be snatched away. He had taken the bait. Now all I had to do was use it to wheedle some answers out of him.

He removed the bifocals and folded them away to re-establish his administrator's composure. "I will need to know the source of the material," he said.

The sprinkler cleared and we resumed our walk. "Doctor Berryman, if you would prefer not to be involved in processing the Scrolls, please say so. I can source translation elsewhere."

He covered a flash of panic with an apologetic smile. "Translation will require a team of experts. Established members of the academic community with reputations to protect. They will require assurance--"

"Professor Eddington must have told you where the Scrolls were stored."

He was too cagey to say anything. That suggested secrets. Benign or malignant I couldn't guess.

"All right, then," I said, "let's get back to the question of what Eddington was doing in the Caucasus Mountains."

"Did he not cover that in his grant application?"

The contents of Eddington's grant application were another nagging question. Falkenberg hadn't shared them with me. He had packed me off to Georgia with a story about evaluating a proposed dig site. Eddington had tried to pass off the Scrolls as a side trip and told me they were none of the Foundation's business but when I got back Falkenberg seemed to know all about them. Including some definite ideas on their subject matter.

"There has been disturbing hyperbole about the Scrolls being used to discredit certain aspects of Judeo-Christian scripture," was all I told Berryman.

He didn't exactly fidget but he could have been more comfortable. "Are you concerned about hysterical publicity?"

"The Foundation sponsors research around the world. We have to deal with diverse belief systems. Religion can fuel disruptive passion."

"I can assure you that Professor Eddington's work was purely scholarly," Berryman said. "Attempts to put it into religious context are misguided."

Eddington himself had mentioned scripture at the dig site. "Could you be more specific?" I asked.

"Professor Eddington's thesis is quite straight-forward," he said. "You are aware of geological findings that the Black Sea came into being only slightly prior to recorded history?"

I remembered the articles vividly. About 7,500 years ago, according to recently uncovered evidence, there had been a hydraulic cataclysm. Seismic activity had split open the Dardanelles and allowed water from the Mediterranean basin to cascade through into the low-lying land beyond. The inrush went on for decades, eventually covering a large lake and several hundred square miles of surrounding ground under what came to be known as the Black Sea. It was one of those gee-whiz discoveries that gave me goose-bumps just to be living at the time when someone figured it out.

"Am I correct in recalling that the inundation has been cited as a possible source of the Biblical tale of the Great Flood?" I asked.

"Baseless conjecture, Mr. Doran."

"What was Eddington's interest?"

"The inundation," Berryman said, "would have driven any lake dwellers to higher ground. Professor Eddington became aware of a former Soviet excavation in the Caucasus Mountains. Like many sites, it is in a series of layers, each successive civilization having built on the ruins of its predecessor. By digging down to the Neolithic level, he hoped to determine whether the site was originally established by people fleeing the inundation."

"Eddington's dig site was a long way from the Black Sea, and quite a way up."

"Today we have the luxury of knowing the boundaries of the Black Sea," Berryman said. "Neolithic tribes watching the incoming water swallow more and more of their land decade after decade had no way to know when or where it would stop. Stronger groups naturally pushed weaker ones to the outer reaches of the new lands."

He had a point but it didn't explain Falkenberg's rant or Eddington's remark. "So you're telling me that if I take a look at the literature, I won't find any Biblical references?"

"Well, of course, there is a general rethinking of history around the early Biblical era."

He threw out a couple of titles on the subject and tried to leave me with the impression that it was all very studious and above-board. I wasn't buying. In the publish-or-perish world of higher learning, the best way to ensure your survival was to become embroiled in a noisy argument. It occurred to me that both Berryman and Eddington might be counting on hysterical publicity to bring the religious academics out swinging.

Change-of-class released a horde of students from the surrounding buildings. Making our way through the bustle gave me a chance to turn Eddington over in my head while I caught up on my girl-watching. Oxford graduates didn't waste time in California party schools. He had come here for one or more reasons that had nothing to do with upgrading Berryman's faculty. His proposed dig site in the Georgian Republic was the real deal; old and heavily guarded. The Alexandria Scrolls also seemed to carry plenty of weight. This brought me to the obvious question.

"You know," I said to Berryman, "Professor Eddington never did get around to telling me what connection the Scrolls had to his theory."

"Quite possibly none. Certainly none that is known. The Scrolls are cipher. They haven't been in the public weal for sixteen centuries."

"Then why is he chasing them?"

"They are a discovery in their own right. If they can be authenticated as artifacts of the Library at Alexandria, they will provide a glimpse into a time and a place we know only from legend."

Where antiquity was concerned, the Library at Alexandria was in the same class as the Hanging Gardens of Babylon and the Colossus of Rhodes. Authentication by a team under Berryman's leadership would guarantee his place in the world of scholarship. He could write his own ticket. He wouldn't have to kiss any more white asses. Particularly if Eddington were never seen nor heard from again, which might explain why Berryman hadn't spent our walk pestering me about what the Foundation was doing to recover the professor he had selected to spearhead his drive for a premier faculty.

I was in no position to criticize. My motives were every bit as tawdry. The biggest thing that ever happened to me was winning the math prize in ninth grade. They had announced my name last, after all the jocks and the debaters and the student leaders. I had flown down to San Sebastian for no better reason than to learn what I had stumbled into and what it might mean for me personally.

Credit for recovering Scrolls from the Library at Alexandria, even just an electronic copy, could conceivably promote me from after-thought to my own footnote in history. Falkenberg would be livid when he found out I had released a copy, but I had risked my neck retrieving the CD and I was entitled to my fifteen seconds in the spotlight. Provided the whole thing wasn't a con. I still had more questions than answers, and the one that nagged me most persistently was how a four-eyed bean counter had wandered into a remote monastery on the coat-tails of a now missing professor and come away with what was beginning to look like the find of the decade. It wouldn't be the first time Owen Doran wound up as a sucker.

"I assume you vetted Eddington pretty carefully before you hired him?" I asked.

"His academic references were impeccable," Berryman assured me as he used a security card to let us into the faculty office building.

"Did he mention why he wanted a posting in California? Granted, you have a fine institution here, but it is half a world away from his research."

"Unfunded research," Berryman said significantly. "It is possible his application grew out of being introduced to your Mr. Falkenberg by Barbara Wren."

"Barbara Wren?"

"She's quite prominent socially," Berryman said. "You may know her name."

"I've met her," I said.

Barbara Wren had been Falkenberg's squeeze before Sofia. I was suddenly very curious what else the relationship might have involved. I collected the file transfer information and spent the taxi ride back to the airport wondering how many knots I could coax out of the Cessna I'd rented for the trip down from San Francisco.

Chapter 4

I had the hotel valet service polish my shoes and press my sport coat and slacks for my appointment with Barbara Wren. Apparently I still wasn't up to the standards of her regular gentleman callers. The security man at her condominium complex used the house phone to make sure I was expected before he let me board the elevator.

Floor numbers lit up in sequence. That was the only hint of movement. The elevator whispered open and let me out into a softly illuminated hallway. A security camera watched me press the button beside Barbara's door. I spent the wait trying to think of something suave to say. The door opened and I forgot how to talk.

I had seen Barbara only on semi-formal occasions but she didn't look much different at home. Short blonde hair swept back with a salon flourish, a silk blouse and straight skirt that flattered her figure without emphasizing or displaying it. She was at no disadvantage without jewelry. Her kind of class grew out of poise, not fashion accessories.

"You're very punctual," she said.

Her tone was always pleasant. It was her eye contact that let you know how well you were scoring. I gave myself four out of a possible ten.

"Thank you for seeing me on such short notice."

She led me into a living room with one of the city's rare unobstructed views of the Bay and installed me on a stylish davenport. Classical music accompanied her to a facing chair. She had once mentioned her favorite piece was Beethoven's *Fur Elise*. Mine was Richie Allen's *Stranger From Durango*.

"I apologize for intruding on your afternoon," I said. "I find myself in an unfamiliar situation. I was hoping you could clarify a few things."

19

She let a smile do her talking. She and I were about the same age but I was on the wrong side of a wide experience gap. That wasn't all bad news. She could have answered my questions on the phone. The fact she was willing to use the million-dollar charm on a non-starter meant she had skin in the game, whatever it was.

"I understand you're acquainted with Professor Eddington?"

Her smile faded into a look of concern. "Were you with him when--?"

"Alex Falkenberg sent me to Georgia to meet him," was all I admitted.

Early on I had felt guilty for abandoning the poor professor. The more I learned, the more sinister Eddington looked and the more cautious I became, particularly around people as smooth as Barbara Wren.

"Poor Roald," she said. "Is there any word?"

I shook my head. The fact that she referred to him by his first name lent some weight to what Berryman had told me.

"Did I hear correctly that you introduced him to Alex Falkenberg?" I asked.

"Roald needed a benefactor to fund his research."

"How long have you known him?"

"He was an acquaintance of my late husband."

Her eyes warned me she didn't like being questioned. She also crossed her legs. I decided to cut to the chase while I was still thinking rationally.

"Did Eddington ever mention anything called the Alexandria Scrolls?"

"Yes," she said, perking up. "Always in the same reverent and mysterious tone."

"Do you recall anything specific?"

"He heard about them from a librarian. A Ms. Czhed."

She spelled it for me. She even knew the D.C. area library where the woman worked. That was too much information. She was putting me on a scent. I didn't know what she expected me to find.

"Had you heard of them prior to Eddington mentioning them?" I asked.

"What is your interest, Owen?"

"I brought back a copy," I said, "or what is purported to be a copy, of the Scrolls."

I had her full attention. I could feel it in ways that had nothing to do with old parchment.

"The copy is on a CD," I said. "I gave the CD to Alex Falkenberg. He was also reverent and mysterious. Which made me curious."

She stood, and half-remembered training aimed at making me a young gentleman brought me to my feet. She plucked a card from a holder on a side table and presented it to me.

"This has my direct number. Please do call if you hear anything about Roald."

My time was up. It was the Scrolls that interested her and as far as she knew Falkenberg had the only copy. I didn't trust myself to handle the situation if she found out I had burned duplicate CDs.

I checked out of my hotel and caught the first available flight back to Seattle to upload a copy of the Scrolls to Berryman's FTP Site before Falkenberg got wind of the transfer.

The Internet summarized the sources Berryman had cited as re-thinking early Bible Era history. The narrative wasn't as flattering as traditional scripture. In the millennium following the inundation that created the Black Sea, the Middle East began to dry up. People had to organize into cities and exploit division of labor to survive, which opened the door for domination by political and religious elites. Domination required muscle and the Biblical Hebrews, according to the theory, were spears for hire who did the dirty work in return for pasture for their flocks, domesticated animals being the wealth of the time.

A tribal uprising ran the Hebrews out of Mesopotamia around 2300 BC. Abraham's gang brought their ill-gotten goats to an area south of the Dead Sea. Herding and farming were never more than part-time gigs, so they hired out to the Egyptians. Over time they acquired too much wealth and power to suit their employers. The Hyksos expulsion left them camped out in the Sinai Desert. With no organized state in the market for their services, they cooked up their own theocracy and took over Canaan.

The theory sounded plausible but the support was more context than evidence. If the Alexandria Scrolls contained proof that the heroes of the Old Testament were just a two-bit militia, the evidence could thin out church collections and keep the peace-loving religions of the world shooting at each other for decades to come. I was imagining what the earnest Presbyterians I had grown up among would think about having *Exodus* turned into a losers-eye view of the bum's rush when the phone rang.

"Owen?"

"Hi, Mom."

I put the phone on speaker and listened through the opening five minutes of why I hadn't called and was I all right and didn't I miss the East coast, which was a polite way of demanding to know when I was coming home.

"You'll never guess who I ran into today."

"Probably not," I agreed.

"You remember Meg Buchanan, don't you?"

Meg Buchanan was impossible to forget. I was fourteen when she moved into the neighborhood. She had the first real set of gonzagas I had seen on someone my age.

"That was a while ago, Mom."

"She was your first crush. I never understood why you couldn't find the courage to ask her to the movies."

Aside from the fact that I was flat out chicken, I got teased enough for having four eyes and two left feet. I wasn't going to invite more by chasing after a girl who couldn't see her shoes without checking a mirror.

"Growing pains, Mom. We all had them. Even you."

"Did you know that her marriage didn't work out?"

"That's too bad," I said.

"She has two lovely boys."

"Mm-hmm."

"They're eight and ten," Mom said hopefully. One more spin on why wasn't I married and where were the grand-kids. "Meg asked about you."

I put it down to polite conversation. Meg Buchanan had no reason to have any personal interest in a doofus she hadn't seen in more than a decade. And she certainly didn't need a third kid to raise.

"Say 'Hi' for me if you see her again," I said.

"Other men are interested."

Mom rattled off a couple of names I remembered vaguely and went on about how well they were doing in their own businesses. Theme number two. Why hadn't I brought my money home and started my own business. Then I could be a real part of the community. Translation: once my assets were at risk, I would be easier to pressure. The end state was a life of quiet desperation. All men needed to be safely pigeon-holed. No square pegs.

That was my deepest dread. I knew the stock option money that paid for my freedom today wouldn't last forever. Someday I would have to go back to counting beans to earn a living. I wondered if the Alexandria Scrolls represented a chance to turn the world on its ear before that happened. Or if they would turn to vapor like a lot of other aspirations before them.

The three hour east coast time difference saved me for now. Mom needled me a little more and called it a night. I mixed a drink.

The phone rang again. I was going to ignore it but caller ID warned me it was Falkenberg. I probably sounded grumpy when I picked up.

"Cheer up, old chum. All's well with the world. You've returned to the Foundation's good graces."

"What are you babbling about?"

"Eddington's back."

"Where?" I felt my hand tighten around the phone.

"Well, not exactly back back, but at least back in civilization."

"Where?" I repeated.

"A hospital in St. Petersburg."

"What did it cost you?"

"No ransom. The Russians recovered him."

"What does recovered mean?"

"Some kind of commando operation," he said. "They aren't publishing the grisly details and I couldn't care less."

"How is he?"

"I don't know, but maybe the State Department will. You and I have an appointment in Washington tomorrow."

"You go," I said. "This sounds like a job for the relentless Falkenberg charm."

"Sorry, old chum. You've been requested by name."

That sounded like trouble. Falkenberg gave me the travel arrangements and hung up without explaining how much or what kind. I was getting an uneasy feeling that my life had just veered off in a very different direction; that the familiar and comfortable past had become irrelevant.

Chapter 5

The flight to D.C. was a lesson in how the rich went in style without shaking any shekels out of the piggy bank. Forget airline fares. Falkenberg called around and found a CEO buddy who had just flown his girl-friend to San Francisco. Falkenberg and I caught the back-haul in the corporate Gulfstream.

Falkenberg was chipper and chatty. "Remember the dance floor I was putting in the beach house?"

I didn't remember the dance floor but Falkenberg's beach house was unforgettable. It dominated a promontory from where it seemed you could look half way to China. The structure had an angular grandeur that might have come from Frank Lloyd Wright; massive enough to swallow a dozen weekend guests and wired with enough high-tech gadgets that Falkenberg could run the place himself when he wanted solitude to do his scheming or pursue his hobbies.

"Ballroom dancing has always been the most elegant of my fantasies," he said.

The image of someone Falkenberg's size tripping the light fantastic belonged in the Sunday comics. The early flight down from Seattle had left me groggy enough to keep a straight face.

"I even had my tailor do up a new tuxedo to break in the floor," he said. "The lady was the perfect complement. Black hair, black velvet gloves half way up from her elbows, black patent leather pumps, black stockings halfway up her thighs."

The residue of perfume in the plane and the memory of Sofia filled out the picture for me.

"How did she hold up the stockings?"

"We live in the age of wonder fabrics, old chum. The real challenge lies in matching patrician curve of face with just the right breast size. Anything less than a C cup degrades the visual experience. Anything larger, well, I can appreciate a D cup as well as the next man if it's properly shaped and supported, but left to the mercy of gravity--"

"You actually spent some money," I said, realizing Sofia couldn't have crammed her rack into C cups with a crowbar, "to hire a sex industry professional for a couple of hours of role playing."

"Fantasy building," he corrected. "The objective is to maintain the romance through climax and the secret is never to engage. Ultimately women will always disappoint. Even if they can suppress their own needs, they will invariably misread some nuance of yours. Send her on her way. The residue of her fragrance and the memory of elegant dance will allow you to finish with the vision gloriously intact."

He closed his eyes and smiled.

We had been acquainted for years, he and I, but he was full of secret places and private thoughts and I had never come to feel that I actually knew him.

Most women would have dismissed him as a chauvinist. They would have missed the point. If he were an auto-erotic and women were no more than sensory stimuli, then they became as fungible as dollar bills. One was as good as another and no woman could ever get her hooks into him.

That raised the question of what Barbara Wren and Sofia expected from him. I could see Falkenberg sporting them as trophies but both struck me as too man-savvy to play that game. At least not for pocket money and party invitations. It also raised the question of whether the concept of fungible people stopped at the gender divide. I didn't want to think about that.

I thought instead about what Falkenberg had told me. Telling people things, snippets of fact or slices of life, was a favorite game of his. The things weren't meant to convey a message as much as to get the listener thinking in a certain direction. Asking for clarification was pointless. He took a perverse delight in responding with silence. It was up to me to divine the meaning behind his lecherous little vignette.

"Now the woman we'll be talking to at the State Department," Falkenberg said, gazing out over the clouds spreading below, "I'm not sure how we should play her."

"If she's a C cup," I said, reclining the seat-back to see if I could manage a few hours sleep before the ordeal, "you can ask her to dance."

She wasn't.

Her name was Rosalinda Baca and she was an ample woman who held court in a smallish interior office in one of the State Department's satellite buildings. An expensive business suit and a framed law degree from Georgetown University did their best to suggest this was only a rung on the ladder to greater things. Lest anyone worry about becoming a victim of her aspirations, she also had pictures of the folks back home to assure her supplicants that she remained grounded in her humble beginnings.

Falkenberg and I sat before her desk appropriately dressed up and buttoned down. Someone who didn't know better might have mistaken us for responsible officers of a substantial foundation. She wasn't impressed. An uncompromising stare made it clear whom she thought was in charge.

"Where," she asked Falkenberg, enunciating each syllable with menacing care, "is Professor Roald Eddington?"

"In a hospital in St. Petersburg," he said, and when her lips compressed in disapproval, added, "So I am told."

"He left the hospital yesterday."

That sounded like a pretty quick recovery for a middle-aged academic who had just survived a two week ordeal at the hands of Chechen bandits and a rescue by Russian commandos. I didn't know whether Falkenberg was thinking the same thing. He just spread his hands.

"Then I don't know where he is."

She rippled meaty fingers on the desk. "I find that most unusual, considering that the Professor has a grant application pending before your Foundation."

"Pardon my curiosity," Falkenberg said, "but why is the U.S. State Department interested in a British citizen last seen in Russia?"

She didn't pardon his curiosity. She gave him a few well chosen words to the effect that he was here to answer questions, not ask them.

I was next on the menu.

She drew herself up in her executive swivel, every inch a Latin matriarch and not a woman to be trifled with.

"You were in Georgia with Professor Eddington."

"Briefly," was all I fessed up to.

Her eyes narrowed to accusing slits. "You brought the Alexandria Scrolls back with you."

"I did not." Moving artifacts across international boundaries without a pile of paperwork was a major no-no.

"You certainly did," she insisted.

"Madam, I have never seen the so-called Alexandria Scrolls. If they in fact exist, and I have no evidence that they do, then they are most probably in the custody of a monastic order of the Georgian Orthodox Church."

"You brought back a CD containing the Scrolls."

A withering glare warned of grave consequences if I tried to deceive her. There were any number of ways she could have known about the CD but the news traveling that fast in official circles left me feeling vulnerable.

"A CD is simply a magnetic medium," I explained. "Polarities are arranged to form a unique sequence of ones and zeros. Machine readable code capable of generating only a pictorial representation. Transfer of a physical artifact is not possible."

"Content is the property of the Government of origin every bit as much as the physical artifact."

Falkenberg cleared his throat. "Ms. Baca, we are not attorneys. If there is a legal matter, perhaps you would be good enough to submit it in writing to the Foundation. I will have it reviewed--"

Indignation began as a red glow at the silk ruff of her blouse and worked its way quickly up to her hairline. "This is the US Department of State. We do not submit anything for the review of private foundations."

Falkenberg just smiled. I knew the smile. He was probably wondering which of his well-placed cronies he could call to get this broad transferred to the horn of Africa.

She focused her fury back on me. "Are you familiar with Interpol?"

"Some sort of international police organization." I recalled them dimly as the people who would send me away for life if I ever duplicated a DVD.

"They have requested an interview with you regarding Professor Eddington's activities."

I had no idea why Interpol or anyone else needed State Department permission to talk to me but any police interest was unwelcome. I had shot my way out of a bandit attack in a foreign country and I hadn't come clean with the authorities.

"I am going to grant that request," she said. "I strongly suggest you be more forthcoming with them than you have been with me."

She opened a Mont Blanc pen and affixed her signature to some paperwork. Her triumphant expression said it all. She had humbled the mighty Falkenberg Foundation and consigned me to people who knew how to deal with disrespectful twerps.

She dismissed us.

We found our way out of the maze of corridors onto a sidewalk crammed with homebound workers.

"Your thoughts," Falkenberg asked as we put up umbrellas against the D.C. drizzle.

"When the facts favor you, pound on the facts. When the law favors you, pound on the law. When neither favors you, pound on the table."

"The Bible," Falkenberg corrected. "Pound on the Bible."

"I didn't see one."

"You weren't supposed to but it was there all the same. Politicians are elected by Evangelicals. When the Bible-bangers complain, State has to dredge their pool of diversity hires and come up with somebody to put on the case."

"What are they complaining about?" I asked as we reached a line of taxis.

"Eddington. The Alexandria Scrolls. They're running scared. Of him, and of what may be in the Scrolls. He's not a citizen. If they can connect him to black market antiquities, they can get his work permit lifted. If they can intimidate the Foundation, they can remove his funding. If they can deadlock the Scrolls in legal limbo, they can keep the contents secret."

"I didn't see much connecting or intimidating or deadlocking. That had to be the shortest interview anyone ever flew across the country for."

"The plane ride was the point," Falkenberg said. "Create any nuisance or expense they can."

"So what's this Interpol business?"

"That's for you and Jerry to find out. While I try to learn what you brought back on that CD."

He got into a taxi and he was gone.

Jerry was Jeremiah Silver, five and a half feet of dithering Juris Doctorate who handled the Foundation's legal affairs and Washington business. He saw me as his prime adversary in an imaginary struggle to become Falkenberg's second in command and eventual successor at the Foundation. I had zero interest in command and doubted that Falkenberg would ever relinquish control over any of his toys. That didn't stop Jerry from hating me with a black passion.

I got into the next cab in line for the ride back to my hotel. I needed a solid dinner, a stiff drink and a good night's sleep. I was already feeling the three hour time difference and I would have more than the police to contend with tomorrow.

Chapter 6

Jerry had changed his hairstyle since I saw him last. He was going with a more conservative trim, as well as more starch in his shirt and probably in his shorts. He was visibly irked when a drop of water from my umbrella landed on his designer glasses.

"Let me do the talking," he instructed as we lined up for security check in the lobby of the building where Interpol had its Washington bureau.

"Jerry, I'll have to say something. I'm the one they want to talk to."

"I'll try to maneuver the questions into yes-no format. The shorter we can keep your answers, the less exposure for the Foundation."

Jerry had a way of making me feel special.

Save for a logo in the reception area, Interpol's office might have belonged to an insurance company. Our interviewer was a bean pole with outsized hands and shirt cuffs turned back over massive forearms. He introduced himself as Inspector Nordheim and seated us at a table in a drab little room.

"I will see some identification, please," he began.

He took a pair of half-spectacles from the pocket of a sweater vest and perched them partway down a hooked beak so he could copy our particulars onto a form. He filled in the blanks with exacting care, as if the work he did now might one day trap us in the lie that would be our undoing. I wondered how much authority he or his organization had.

"What exactly is Interpol?" I asked.

He peered at me over the top of his glasses, seemingly unsure whether I was ignorant or just needling him.

"I mean I sort of know but I don't really," I said.

29

He gave me an abridged and impatient version. Organization of police agencies, cooperation across national boundaries, you can run but you can't hide. When he was finished I had no more clue what they could do to me than I had when he started.

"What did Professor Eddington tell you about the death of Sebastian Eglik?" he asked.

The question blind-sided me. I had come to deny accusations that I had smuggled artifacts. Nordheim seemed to have something more sinister in mind.

"Who?" I asked.

"A dealer in stolen antiquities," he said in a voice that warned me not to be coy with him. "Advisory circulars have been widely distributed."

Jerry demanded proof that the Falkenberg Foundation had received copies. Nordheim repeated what he had said. Jerry informed him that was not satisfactory and used his razor point pen to make and underline a note on a yellow legal tablet.

"What is the relationship of Professor Eddington to this man Eglik?" Jerry asked.

Nordheim spun us a grisly story that went well with the chilly droplets of sweat making their way down my spine. Turkish police had found a corpse with no head and no hands, but nothing stops CSI Istanbul. The heft of the torso matched a criminal named Eglik, a Muslim with a strong religious yen to be buried intact. So strong that he saved extracted teeth. One was ground up for DNA, which was matched to the dead man. The last name in Eglik's appointment book was Roald Eddington.

Jerry was still writing while he asked, "Is Professor Eddington suspected of involvement?"

"Beheading is a Muslim signature," Nordheim said. "As is removal of the hands of thieves. You have received circulars on The Scalded Woman?"

Jerry demanded proof of delivery. Nordheim kept the story terse. Some years ago a gang active in antiquities traffic was run to ground in a villa in a Tehran suburb. The leader was killed in the ensuing gun battle. The youngest of his wives was scalded when a samovar went over in the fracas. She managed to escape and took control.

"Some details may be apocryphal," Nordheim conceded. "Muslim society does not encourage women to lead, and no hospital admissions were reported for scalding. Nevertheless, the group became known as The Scalded Woman."

"That," Jerry declared, "does not concern the Falkenberg Foundation."

Nordheim thumped two thick fingers on the table. "These Alexandria Scrolls, they are behind this business. The fact that Eglik's old Oxford crony Eddington was in Istanbul at the time proves the connection."

I was thoroughly confused. "Oxford crony?" was all that came out of my mouth.

Nordheim was suspicious. He watched for any glimmer of recognition while he told the rest of the tale. Eglik was the son of a Turkish smuggler and a British school teacher who insisted on an English education. Mom passed away and dad pulled young Sebastian out of Oxford and finagled him a commission in the Turkish paratroops to toughen him up to take over the family business. Apparently it hadn't toughened him enough to deal with the gang Nordheim called The Scalded Woman. The gang was after the Scrolls, and when Eddington went to Istanbul to enlist Eglik's help in obtaining them, the gang killed Eglik as a warning.

"Your foundation is circulating copies for scholarly authentication to support the bids that will be demanded on the black market," Nordheim finished.

"Digital copies," I corrected, to be sure he understood no actual artifacts were involved.

"Which you obtained from a Georgian monastery."

"And which the Foundation is circulating for legitimate scholarly purposes."

"And these Georgian monks, they turned over to you, a complete stranger, an item of such value for what reason?"

I didn't have an answer for him. Worse, I didn't have one for myself.

Jerry waved me to silence. "Under American law," he warned Nordheim, "burden of proof rests with the accuser."

"I have written permission from the State Department to conduct this interview," Nordheim retorted.

The discussion went downhill from there. Nordheim had already made up his mind that criminal elements were using the Falkenberg Foundation to bring the Scrolls to America for sale on the black market and he wasn't going to let two underweight twits get in the way of proving it. The Foundation was Jerry's meal ticket and he wasn't going to let any sanctimonious official threaten it. They spent the better part of an hour ranting at each other. I was glad to finally get out of there.

Jerry insisted we go to his office and prepare a report for Falkenberg. Between Nordheim's information and my experience in the Caucasus Mountains, it was obvious that there was more than a just a little academic intrigue swirling around the Alexandria Scrolls. Survival instinct suggested that I find out what was really going on before I became a target again. I told Jerry to stick his report where the sun didn't shine and caught a cab.

Barbara Wren told me the existence of the Scrolls was uncovered by a Ms. Czhed, who worked in a D.C. library. The building didn't qualify as historic, but it was old enough to have one escalator shut down for maintenance and sheets of plywood walling off spot repairs. I made my way to the reference section, a large island set squarely in the main traffic pattern.

A woman was in charge there. Lack of a well-defined chin combined with loose folds of skin at her throat made her look older than the fifty odd years I guessed from her eyes. A name plaque identified her as Beatte Czhed.

"Is there somewhere we could speak privately?" I asked when she had read the Foundation card I'd handed her.

"I'm afraid not." She glanced at the people lined up at computer screens. They were her flock and couldn't be abandoned. "Is there something I can help you find?"

"It's about the Alexandria Scrolls," I said.

Her eyes shifted around the room. Who or what she was looking for I didn't know. All I had was a scrap of information that obviously had been dropped to steer me here.

"Barbara Wren said you were the one who told Professor Eddington about the Scrolls."

"Roald is a fool," she said quietly and passionately, "if he thinks a woman like Barbara Wren would have him."

Embarrassment colored her face and she moved off to answer a question for an animated Korean with a wispy goatee. I probably shouldn't have expected much. Walking in off the street and finding her in less than a minute had used up my entire quota of luck for the next several months. There was nothing to do but wait.

She didn't come back until it became clear that I wasn't going away on my own. "I really don't want to discuss it."

"The Foundation has a copy of the Scrolls."

What little chin she had quivered and she stared at me with eyes that didn't dare believe what I was saying.

"Translation has been commissioned, of course, but to establish provenance we also need to trace the movement of the Scrolls from source."

She swiveled one of the computers to check the internet and make sure the Falkenberg Foundation existed. I did my best to look like my picture on the web site.

"How did you learn about the Scrolls?" I asked.

"I happened on the story when I was researching my masters thesis," she said, sounding defensive, as if I had accused her of something. "I had planned to write it on the destruction of the Library at Alexandria."

"Could you tell me how the Scrolls wound up in a monastery in the Georgian Republic?"

"In 330 A.D. the country of Georgia, the old Kingdom of Colchis, converted to Orthodox Christianity," she said, and went on to explain that conversion presented a problem. The Georgian language is unique, being neither Slavic nor Indo-European, so there were no religious texts available in the native tongue. Monks were dispatched to bring back texts for translation. She said there was a group in Alexandria in A.D. 391 when the Byzantine Emperor Theodosius ordered the Library destroyed. That didn't square with what I had learned in history class.

"Excuse me," I interrupted, "I thought the Library was burned by Caesar's Legions before the birth of Christ."

She gave me a pitying look. "The Library was located in the Royal Compound, which served as the main Roman fortification during the siege of Alexandria."

She made short work of the notion that a General of Caesar's skill and experience would have lost his position to fire, intentional or accidental, and went on with her story. The Georgian monks slipped into the Library posing as part of a vandal mob and spirited away a hundred scrolls. I had a mental image of hooded figures, guttering torches and groping shadows.

"So the Library was destroyed in A.D. 391," I said.

"Some damage was reported to the Serapeum, but actual destruction was unlikely, since a later claim had a Caliph destroying it in A.D. 672. The source was famously anti-Muslim so the claim is questionable but it would not have been useful even as slander if the Library were not only operating but widely known at the time."

She glanced around at her own decaying surroundings. "The most likely fate of the Library is that it simply fell into disuse and disrepair as

Egypt and Alexandria slipped further into the backwaters of culture and commerce. It died a slow death of scholarly neglect."

"The Scrolls," I decided, "never came to public attention because your thesis was never accepted. No academic advisor would sign off on a document that took responsibility for the Library's destruction away from a vandal army and laid it at the feet of his scholastic predecessors."

"I should have left well enough alone."

"The Scrolls could re-write history," I said.

"All the Scrolls have done is attract people like that Mr. Manders," she said with no small distaste.

"Mr. Manders?"

"He came here one day. That harridan brought him. He railed about the Scrolls and demanded I tell him where Roald was. He threatened me when I told him I didn't know. Security had to remove him."

My interest in Manders spiked. He sounded like someone who could shed some light on the criminal activity around the Scrolls.

"Did Manders leave contact information?"

"Why?"

"It's important that I find him. Any threat to the Scrolls is a threat to our efforts."

All she had for me was a wan smile. "People like you and me will never be credited for our work. We don't have scholarly credentials."

She moved off to help the line of people that had formed at the counter. Normally she would be right. The two of us would never be anything but faceless drones. I was counting on the Scrolls to change the odds in my favor. I had a sense that she was too. In spite of anything she said. I stood my ground.

After about fifteen minutes she put the line on hold and went to her desk. She brought me a piece of paper with an address block printed on it. I thanked her and left.

The address was in Virginia. The map I consulted over lunch suggested I might be able to make it there and back in an afternoon. I hoped Mr. Manders and his harridan weren't as fearsome as Ms. Czhed thought they were.

Chapter 7

I had always imagined rural Virginia as upper crust horse farms where bureaucrats and their toadies frittered away my tax money. I shoe-horned myself into a rental car and got an education.

The generic suburban sprawl south of D.C. thinned gradually into rolling fields. I passed the occasional Civil War monument but there wasn't a thoroughbred or white rail fence in sight. Crossroads towns came infrequently; clusters of buildings where churches stood on prominent corners and Toyotas outnumbered Fords. Schizophrenic blends of quaint Americana and world culture not unlike the town in upstate New York where the Doran family hailed from.

The map directed me onto two lane blacktop that wound into hillier and less inviting surroundings. Thickets of brambles supported rotted fences. An unpaved track sloped down into a hollow. If it hadn't been for a name lettered on a mailbox I never would have found the Manders residence. The house was ramshackle and unpainted. Any neighbors were well out of sight. I parked between a rusted Chevy pick-up and a discarded refrigerator in what passed for a front yard.

The dog went nuts as soon as I got out of the car. It wasn't any breed I recognized. Just something gigantic crossed with something vicious. A length of chain was all that kept it from turning me into geek burger. I gave it a wide berth making for the porch.

A woman was waiting for me. She stood just inside a screen door. It remained hooked. Opening it would have required taking one of her talons off the shotgun she held. Bones were prominent under a faded print dress and a baggy sweater. Unbrushed hair straggled down on either side of a thin face. Compressed lips and cagey eyes didn't make her a harridan, but they were a good start on the stereotype. I hoped my smile didn't look as nervous as it felt.

"Mrs. Manders?" I inquired. "Mrs. Lew Manders?"

"Who's asking?"

"My name is Owen Doran." I held up a business card.

She peered at it through the screen. "Whatta you want?"

"I'd like to talk to Mr. Manders. Is he in?"

"What about?"

"The Alexandria Scrolls."

She stepped back and leveled the shotgun. "Clear off!"

"Let him in," came a loud male voice from somewhere in the house.

"Go to hell," she croaked over her shoulder.

"This is hell. Let him in."

She took one claw off the shotgun just long enough to unhook the screen door. I opened it carefully, cringing when the hinges squeaked, and stepped into a dim hallway.

The house had a distinctive aroma; the tang of hot smoke leaking from a wood stove and the sweetish smell of too many apples stored in one place: not unpleasant but different enough to make me feel alien; a trespasser in a place I didn't know or understand.

Mrs. Manders jerked her head at a doorway. "Well, you want to talk to him, don't you?"

The doorway let me into a barren parlor. Lew Manders sat in a wheel chair. Light through a curtained window showed touches of gray in his untrimmed hair and beard stubble. He wore a flannel shirt buttoned over long underwear. A blanket covered what remained of his lower body. He seemed to be missing all of one leg and part of another. He took a pistol from under the blanket.

"I could kill you," he said.

I recognized the pistol from the six o-clock news. It was a military issue automatic. I had never seen a real one before, let alone had one pointed at me.

"Kill you where you stand," he said.

Standing wasn't something I could take for granted. The legs that had brought me into the room had been none too steady and looking into the muzzle of Manders' automatic was quickly reducing them to rubber. The only place to sit was a threadbare armchair, so I sat there.

Manders didn't like that. "Tell the cops you were one of those home invaders. That's what I'd tell them. Law couldn't touch me. Couldn't do a damn thing to me."

The place wasn't worth invading. Floorboards were visible where the carpet had worn through. The few pieces of unmatched furniture looked to have been refinished more than once. The small fireplace was cold for lack of wood and a Coleman lantern on the mantle testified to the lack of electric service. I saw nothing that would connect Lew Manders with anything as exotic as the Alexandria Scrolls.

"I thought you wanted to talk," I said.

"Never said so."

"You told her to send me in. I thought you wanted to talk about the Alexandria Scrolls."

He eyed me closely, licked his lips. "You bring anything to drink?"

I shook my head.

"Maybe you don't hold with it?" he asked.

"I could use a stiff one myself," I admitted.

"She don't hold with it," he said in a voice loud enough to carry. "Been more'n a year since I've had so much as a taste."

He didn't get a rise from his wife, wherever she had gotten off to, and he probably hadn't expected to.

"Seems like nobody holds with it," he said. "All well and fine to send Lew Manders off to do your dirty work, but when the time comes to give him a little something to ease the pain afterward, nobody holds with it."

"The Alexandria Scrolls?" I asked, glancing at the wheel chair where his legs would have been.

"Lost them in the national security."

He waved his gun at the wall to prove his point. A few cheaply framed photographs hung there. A portrait of a younger Lew Manders in an Army uniform. A news clipping of a large military formation. A few snapshots of soldiers in the field. Not the shrine some veterans make to their military careers. No Sergeant's stripes. No commendations. Just a few random memories. And a suggestion that twenty years ago Manders might have seen enlistment as a way out of grinding poverty.

"Grenades going off rapid fire," he said. "Boom, boom, boom. I was the only one made it out. Only one made it to a hospital."

A bad case of nerves had my brain in overdrive and it generated something that might have qualified as inspiration. Manders' description of rapid fire grenades fit pretty well with the explosive warheads of a 37 millimeter antiaircraft gun. It was easy to picture him disenchanted with military enlistment, taking work as a security contractor in a remote corner of the world, falling in with other men of the same character. The sort of men who might be hired to drive to the monastery, do a number on the religious pussies and make off with the Scrolls.

Who might have hired them or how the monks would have known they were coming I couldn't guess but the events were easy to visualize. A truck big enough to cart off a hundred scrolls would have to move slowly in the mountain pass. It would have been a turkey shoot.

"Hospital," Manders repeated. "Goddamn butcher shop, that's what. They took both my legs. I seen guys get around pretty good on just one. Crutches and one good foot to plant. They took both mine."

I decided to check on my theory. "Well, a third world hole like the Georgian Republic, what can you expect?"

Malice narrowed his eyes. "You got a cell phone?"

Like a doofus I started to reach for it.

"Call Eddington," he ordered. "Tell him to get his fat ass down here."

"Eddington is out of the country," I said, and wondered what it would feel like when Manders shot me.

"Where," he demanded.

"I last saw him in the Georgian Republic."

"Then you get your ass back where you come from. You get hold of Eddington. You tell him they're going to kill him."

"Sure." Messenger sounded better than corpse. "Who is going to kill him?"

"He gets that when he comes down here and kisses my ass. And forks over cash while he's doing it. Forks over until I tell him it's okay to stop."

"Someone is going to kill him over the Scrolls?" I asked.

"Fuckin' A they are. Now get out of my old lady's chair. Get out of my place."

I didn't need to be told twice.

Mrs. Manders was waiting for me outside. She stood by the rental car with her shotgun, blocking the driver's door.

"I oughtta have some money," she told me. "Letting you see him like I did. I oughtta have some money for that."

Offering some seemed pointless. She would only demand more.

"What about me?" I asked.

That surprised her. The shotgun sagged in her grasp.

"I paid down good dollars for that rental car to drive all the way out here," I said.

"I oughtta have some dollars," she insisted.

"For him and his stupid talk about national security?"

The dog had quit testing the limits of its chain and settled down to a routine of prowling and growling. I glanced in both directions and lowered my voice to a conspiratorial register.

"What's he holding back for?" I asked. "Doesn't he want to make money?"

Greed warred with suspicion in her eyes. I moved close enough to smell her nicotine addiction.

"What did he tell you?"

"Told me I oughtta marry him up," she said. "Said he was getting a big disability. Said I better marry him up before some other woman got him away from me."

"Disability?" I asked. "From where?"

"Wasn't none. I'm his disability. Me. That's all there is."

Her laugh was a dispirited cackle. At least she seemed to have given up on the idea of shaking me down. I climbed into the rental car and got out of there before it dawned on her she could shave a little off the pet food bill by shooting me and feeding me to the Hound of the Baskervilles.

Adrenaline drained out of my system and left me shivering on the drive back to D.C. How much of Lew Manders' rant I should take seriously I didn't know but I couldn't deny what I had seen. Two people who couldn't afford to feed a canary kept a watchdog that was probably eating them out of house and home. Both kept guns handy even when they weren't expecting company. Someone or something had put the fear of God into them. I had a sneaking suspicion Falkenberg knew who or what it was and had deliberately not told me. I dug out my phone and hit the speed dial.

Falkenberg didn't answer his cell number. It was past five but I tried Jerry's office anyway. The receptionist was still there. She told me Jerry and Falkenberg were in conference and couldn't be disturbed. I would be waiting when they got out.

Chapter 8

Jerry Silver's receptionist was Catherine Morse. While Jerry merely detested me, she held me in utter contempt. Twerps of my ilk were beneath the dignity of an elegant creature who had married a third generation Annapolis graduate; galling reminders of how cruelly life had treated her. She should be an Admiral's Lady, hosting military soirees and attending a-list parties instead of staffing the front desk of a small law office to help finance the kids' college tuition while her hero pushed paper as deputy something-or-other at a supply depot in Maryland.

I knew about her aspirations only because I had overheard her mention them to Falkenberg in a voice that suggested there might be something spicy in it for him if he used his connections help them along. Falkenberg declined politely enough but politeness didn't count when you were turning down that kind of an offer.

"What's the meeting about?" I asked to give her a chance for a little payback.

"That," she informed me, "is confidential."

Apparently I was even farther down her list of scum than Falkenberg. I sat down to wait.

Five men's umbrellas in the stand meant the conference had been in session since before the rain had stopped earlier in the afternoon. The three men who finally came out with Falkenberg and Jerry ran to a pattern. They had the air of academic leaders, the sort who would step to a podium and address a room full of professors on any excuse. Falkenberg wasn't just recruiting scholars to translate the Alexandria Scrolls. He was assembling a sales force to evangelize the translation.

"…must be presented as a whole," one was emphasizing. He stood over six feet, still slim and strong at fifty, an open collar dress shirt under his sport coat, full hair combed straight back and horn-rimmed spectacles.

The next to put in his two cents was a peppery sort in a yellow polka dot bow tie. "The Gnostic Gospels found at Nag Hammadi in 1945 came to prominence because they provided a fully flowered augmentation to the New Testament."

"Fragments," the third opined, making too much of an Irish brogue, "raise more questions then they answer."

"We see eye to eye," Falkenberg assured them.

He ushered them out of the office with smiling good-byes. The instant they were gone his face turned to stone. He jerked his head for me and Jerry to follow and strode back to the conference room. Jerry shut the three of us inside.

"Berryman!" Falkenberg bellowed.

He loomed close, riveting my eyes with a look that demanded of full confession of my sins. It was theater. I had seen too many years of it to be impressed. I helped myself to one of the leather chairs at Jerry's glass topped conference table to wait him out.

Falkenberg began pacing. "I move heaven and earth to persuade top ivy-league academics to take the Alexandria Scrolls for translation and they tell me that a copy has already gone to some diversity hire at a California backwater."

"Eddington is a member of Berryman's faculty," I pointed out.

Falkenberg withdrew a folded sheet from his pocket saying, "this turned up in my e-mail. I was on the cc: line," and shook it open with a flourish.

"My dear Berryman," he read aloud, mocking Eddington's Oxford drawl. "I was thrilled beyond words to learn that you have come into possession of a soft copy of the Alexandria Scrolls. My only regret is that I will not be able to join you at once in the adventure of translation. I am close to agreement with the monks to allow radio-carbon dating of the binding wood, as well as bits of leather said to be relics of the original containers. I must remain in Georgia to complete the arrangements. Meanwhile I urge you to spare no effort nor tolerate any obstacle. Godspeed. Eddington."

I was busted.

Falkenberg folded the printout away. "You sold me out," he said with a disbelieving shake of his head. "Gave Berryman a copy to make your own name."

"You sent me to Georgia with half a story and damn near got me killed."

"I ought to sack you for disloyalty."

The threat told me that my position was safe for the moment, even if I wasn't. If he actually meant to sack me, he wouldn't have beaten around the bush. If he didn't mean to sack me, he probably had something worse in mind.

"What you ought to do," I said, "is tell me everything you know, or think you know, about Eddington and the Scrolls."

He plopped his bulk into a chair and let out a snort. "I know you came up a tad short, Owen, old chum. I had already sent a copy of your CD to each of the three men I spoke with today. They all came to the same count. Fifty seven separate documents."

I let an impatient stare do my talking.

"According to history," Falkenberg said, "the monks recovered one hundred scrolls from Alexandria. Now, in your professional accountant's opinion, what is the difference between fifty seven and one hundred?"

"Leave auditing to the people who are trained for it," I said sourly.

"Oh." He glanced at Jerry. "Do I have my numbers wrong?"

Jerry didn't say a word. He was enjoying my skewering.

"First," I said, enumerating the flaws any bean counter would notice, "unless you are holding out on me, you have no source document."

I paused to give him a chance to one-up me, but he either had nothing or he wasn't biting so I pushed on.

"Second, one hundred is a round number. Never trust a round number. Third, even if that is the number of scrolls the God squad filched from the Serapeum, they had to transport them more than a thousand miles under primitive conditions. Any number could have been lost in transit. Fourth, we're talking about animal hides that have been decaying for sixteen centuries. A one hundred percent survival rate isn't likely."

Falkenberg didn't like arguments. Particularly logical ones. His knee jerk reaction was to talk fast in a voice loud enough to beat the offender into submission.

"Get your head out of your textbooks," he ordered. "Look at the real facts." He stood and resumed pacing. "A church struggling to survive in a stone broke Republic. Scrolls worth a small fortune on the black market. Obvious ploy: cull out the religious writings, the ones that could knock the props out from under their gig, and foist off a copy of the rest on some gullible foundation for translation to whet collectors' appetites."

At least some of that had come from Jerry's notes from Interpol. Jerry had his two cents to put in.

"Alex, their motives in culling the religious scrolls needn't have been sinister. They may just have wanted to avoid selling icons of the faith."

Either way the conclusion was the same. Friar Bones knew a sucker when he saw one, and when he saw Owen Doran he thought he'd died and gone to heaven. He'd sold me the CD, fixed me up with the Luger and the hash to increase my chances of getting it back to civilization and turned a tidy profit at the Foundation's expense.

"This time," Falkenberg said, "I'll be going with Owen to make sure we get the whole collection. Originals. No copies."

Jerry wasn't as panic-prone as I was but that was enough to drain his face of color. "Alex, a digital copy is one thing, but if you touch the actual Alexandria Scrolls, it would take an act of Congress to keep you out of prison."

"All right. Draft one."

Jerry just stared.

"There's a twelve hundred page pork bill up for vote in two weeks," Falkenberg reminded him. "Draft a couple of paragraphs giving the Foundation specific authority to pursue and recover the Alexandria Scrolls and exempting us from any existing statutes to the contrary. We'll have one of our friends in the House slip it in. It'll be signed into law before anyone is the wiser."

"Alex, you're talking about using the signature of the President of the United States to authorize a treasure hunt."

"The office pays four hundred thousand dollars a year," Falkenberg said. "It's about time at least one of the occupants did something to earn it."

Private bills like the one Falkenberg proposed were legal. I recalled reading somewhere that about a hundred of them went through Congress every year. Jerry was probably on intimate terms with the process. From the look on his face, it scared him thoroughly. Although not quite as thoroughly as the idea of going back into Georgia scared me.

"Given my current standing with the State Department," I put in, "I don't think I could get a visa to Disneyland."

"Fill out the paperwork before you leave D.C. I'll call a couple of people who can help Jerry shepherd your application through."

"There's something else you should know before you make any rash decisions," I said.

I told them about my visit to Mr. and Mrs. Manders. Jerry took his usual copious notes. He did an unusual amount of underlining.

Falkenberg's eyes lit up. "So you think this Manders character was hired to raid the Monastery and steal the Scrolls?"

"I thought you might know," I said in a voice that betrayed my fading hope of learning anything.

Ideas tumbled out of Falkenberg's mouth as fast as he could form them. "Eddington needed to establish himself with the Georgian Orthodox Church. He had to gain their trust if he was going to broker the Scrolls. So he heard about a raid--no, better still--he commissioned a raid. Either he hired the thugs himself or he went to the Evangelicals who want to destroy the Scrolls and conned them into it. Then he ratted out his own conspiracy to get in good with the Orthodox Church. That's how he got access to the monastery."

"Alex," Jerry warned, "this could be serious."

"It is serious," I put in, remembering Lew Manders' missing legs.

"I told both of you when you signed on that this job would take guts," Falkenberg said.

The Foundation was Jerry's livelihood. All he could do was try not to swallow his Adam's apple.

"And you?" Falkenberg demanded of me.

Until now, I had seen the Foundation as a harmless adventure. The Scrolls changed everything. Shadowy writings stolen from the legendary Library at Alexandria sixteen hundred years ago. Perhaps the discovery of the century. Certainly the biggest thing that would ever happen in my life. And the most dangerous.

"It can't hurt to look," I said, hoping it was true but knowing from experience that anything Falkenberg said was just a façade for the scheming that was really going on in his mind.

Chapter 9

Falkenberg's three wise men haunted me on plane ride back to Seattle. I had risked my neck recovering a copy of the Scrolls and they knew more about the contents than I did. Comprehensive translation would require a platoon of PhDs, but I had an Internet full of Greek reference material to add to the elementary texts left over from my college electives. It was time to get at least a general idea what the reams of old writing said.

The standard approach to translation was to lay out the work in a grid, with one word to each cell. The first page took hours in front of a computer, cutting and pasting. The densely packed text contained over four hundred words. After a day of exasperating trial and error, I arrived at a best guess for eleven of them. My talents, assuming I had any, appeared to lie elsewhere.

The phone rang while I was packing it in. Caller ID showed Falkenberg's San Francisco number so I picked up.

"Owen," I said.

"This is Sofia."

There was no mistaking the voice. It conjured up her image in a midnight blue cocktail sheath and filled the room with a memory of head-spinning fragrance.

"You have forgotten?" she asked.

The only things I had forgotten were the impromptu lines I had rehearsed for the next time I talked to her.

"I remember," was all I could choke out.

"I will be in Seattle tomorrow afternoon. I must stay one night. It is all right if I stay with you?"

"Sure." Given my limited experience with drop-dead gorgeous chicks asking to spend the night, I was lucky to articulate even one word.

She gave me her flight number and arrival time and told me how much she was looking forward to seeing me again. It took all the composure I could muster to exchange pleasant good-byes with her.

Just picking her up would be humbling. My Honda was as pristine as an obsessive-compulsive bean counter could keep it, but it was also ten years old. Renting something snazzy was pointless. Falkenberg owned a fleet of exotic iron. After a sleepless night the only strategy I came up with was to mind my manners and try to keep from pegging her creep meter. I made sure I got to the terminal early.

Disembarking passengers came in waves, disgorged by shuttles from the satellite gates. Sofia was easy to spot. She moved in the crowd with the ease of drifting smoke. Her outfit was upscale and demure; slacks, turtleneck, sport jacket. She wore an ornate headscarf, the kind I had seen in Muslim countries where women had to craft fashion from required coverage.

"Hello, Owen."

Her smile was friendly and no more, which allowed me to maintain enough poise to return her greeting. Escorting her to baggage claim started my blood boiling toward panic. Until her call she had been a distant fantasy, shielded and unreachable behind Falkenberg's money. Pointing out her suitcase she was real and immediate. Walking out to the car I knew I would have to come out of my shell and muster some snippets of social conversation.

"It's past five," I said as I eased the Honda out into rush hour traffic. "I thought we could stop somewhere for dinner. What do you like?"

"You have natural food store where you live?"

"Sure."

So much for conversation. The traffic took us north onto on Interstate 405. Sofia was silent, watching the passing commercial landscape.

"Once there were farms here," she decided.

Japanese truck farms, before World War II's greatest generation thought up dispossession and internment. Now it was all tilt-ups, diesel semi-tractors and 737s. I had learned about the farms from a pictorial history I had snatched impulsively off a supermarket rack. How Sofia knew they had been there was beyond me.

When we got to the store, she cruised the produce aisles. Very little of what she selected was packaged. I swiped my credit card at checkout, loaded her loot into the Honda and wound up into the suburban hills wondering how someone accustomed to the best would react to a tract house with a sliver view and do-it-yourself landscaping.

"Oh, you have a cat!" she exclaimed as soon as I let her in.

Actually Luther belonged to the neighbors. I didn't know how the little burglar could get into a completely locked house but he liked to sun himself in my bay window. I left Sofia with him and took her bag to the spare bedroom.

Unlike me, Luther knew how to handle chicks. When I returned to the living room he was laying on his back on Sofia's lap having his tummy rubbed. I was pretty sure I wouldn't be getting that kind of treatment. I still had no clue why she had come and no bright ideas how to put the question to her.

"Cook first or talk first?" I asked.

Vintage Owen Doran. Blunt and straight to the point. If Sofia was miffed, she didn't show it.

"Cook first," she said, and put Luther aside to go powder her nose.

She came back without the head-scarf and the sport jacket. The straight black hair and the drop-dead figure were exactly as I remembered. Focusing on dinner would be a challenge.

She knew her way around a kitchen, handling a knife like a professional chef; holding it at the balance, fingers of her free hand against the blade, slicing and dicing vegetables as fast as my eyes could follow. She was making a dinner salad and asked if I wanted one. Not being fond of rabbit food, I declined politely and tried to stay out of her way while I cooked a piece of steak and baked a potato. My sole inspiration was to put something romantic on the CD player to accompany the meal.

"Do you have any favorite music?" I asked.

She ransacked my eclectic collection and found what she wanted. I never would have seen her as the type for Muddy Waters, T-Bone Walker and John Lee Hooker.

"You and Alexander," she said as we set two places at the dining room table, "you are very different."

Since she probably had Falkenberg figured out already, I assumed she was nominating the life story of Owen Doran as dinner conversation. Telling even the summary version was an exercise in humility. Middle kid sandwiched between two sisters. One lived in Tampa, the other in Dallas. Mom still kept the old house at 1247 Spruce Street and worked as a teller for the regional bank where my father worked for thirty seven years.

Dad had risen to assistant branch manager. They found him dead of a stroke in the glorified broom closet they gave him for an office. He was a good guy and they said nice things about him at the memorial service but it all boiled down to he was born, he lived, he died. He had set the standard of dullness and I had followed in his footsteps. Out of it and proud of it.

"I worked for Alex in a high-tech start-up," I said. "He was going somewhere and I wasn't, so I climbed aboard for the ride."

"Why are you the one he trusts?" she asked.

"Those days are past," I said. If they ever existed.

She shook her head. "Past, today and always. You are the one he calls when something matters to him."

That surprised me enough to shut me up. We ate to the strains of *Stormy Monday*. She used the European knife and upside down fork style, working her way through a salad that would have passed muster in Paris.

"You have never married," she said.

That was probably obvious to any woman.

"Husband material," I said defensively, "isn't the way awkward men like to see themselves."

"Do you really think you are awkward?" she asked. "Or do you just say that so I will not expect so much from you?"

"If I deny the obvious, I'll just look ridiculous."

"Do you want adventure?" she asked.

I defined adventure the way most people did: thrills with no real danger. Her steady blue eyes suggested she wasn't talking about the OSHA approved version. She looked like she could face down the real deal. My grin felt sheepish.

"Do you know what a yellow streak is?"

"If it keeps you from returning to the Georgian Republic, it is a good thing."

I had the impression we had come to the real reason for her visit. I waited for her to elaborate.

"I'm flattered by your interest," I said when she didn't. "I don't understand it, but I'm flattered."

"I like you. Not in the way that I want you to use me. But I think you are a good person. I don't want to see you hurt."

And in the 'nice guys finish last' category, once again we have Owen Doran. Not that I thought I had any real chance. I just wasn't used to being deflated so abruptly.

She was done with the salad and she got up and took her plate into the kitchen. I collected the rest of the dishes and followed. The night I met her I'd been full of questions about who and what she was, but those were the curiosity of a roving male eye. Now my need to know was a lot more personal.

"I've told you everything that's worth knowing about me," I said. "I know nothing about you."

"Owen, you do not know what is worth knowing about you. You have not lived enough to find out. That much I can tell from the way you talk about yourself."

"Even if that's true, it doesn't answer the question."

"Do not ask me to tell you what you do not want to hear."

"It can't be that bad."

Solemn eyes said otherwise. "You will not want me here when you have heard it."

"I said you can stay the night. You can stay. No matter what you tell me."

"It is not that you will lock me out of your house. You will lock me out of your soul. That is the kind of person you are. You are quiet. You live inside yourself. You will not argue. You will simply lock out anything you do not like."

She had figured me out pretty quickly. Not that I was that mysterious.

"You liked me when you first saw me," she said. "I want you to like me when I leave. I don't want to be locked out."

"You'll have to take the risk," I said. "I don't know who you are, so I don't have anyone to let in."

She thought about it for a minute, another person who lived inside and locked out the people and things she didn't want to deal with. I could see in her eyes that something was boiling up under the lid. I wasn't sure whether she was going to cry but even the possibility was startling.

"I will tell you," she decided. "I will tell you and then maybe you will despise me so much it will keep you out of Georgia and that will make it worth the cost."

Chapter 10

Sofia took time to brew a cup of aromatic tea. She sat at one end of the sofa, slipping off her shoes and curling her legs under her. Cuba Libre was my after dinner drink and her somber expression made me wonder if I might really need it tonight. I sat at the opposite end of the sofa, where I wouldn't crowd her.

Luther came back from his own dinner. Ever the gentleman, he meowed for permission before he hopped up onto her lap. She put her tea aside and stroked his fur.

"I am born in Moldova," she said. "Do you know where that is?"

"East Central Europe?" I ventured.

"I live there on a farm and each day I must walk to the village to go to school. Sometimes men come in a car and tell the girls they can be waitresses in the west and earn money. We are warned about such men and I try to run but they are very fast and they grab me into the car and take me away."

I knew what was coming next. It didn't matter that I didn't want to hear it. I had already let the genie out of the bottle.

"They want to use me," she said. "I say no and fight and they use me anyway. They keep me in a dark room and they come often. If I say no, they starve me and use me. If I say yes, they just use me. Just being used is not so bad as being starved and used and that is how they teach me to always say yes."

There was no emotion in her voice. No simmering anger. No whine of helplessness. Not even a hint of resignation. As if she had walled it off into the past and were talking about another Sofia.

"I am taken to Israel," she said. "I am sold to a place where men pay to use me. One night the police come and the place is closed and I am sold again and taken to Rome. I am sold to all the great religious places. From the street where I have to wait for men I can see the Vatican. I see the lights and I think it must be warm there but I can only shiver and wait for the next man."

A stiff belt of my Cuba Libre stabilized my outlook a little. "But you've gotten away from that now. It's all behind you."

"One night I am told not to go the street. I am stripped naked and taken to a room. I expect a man but a woman is waiting. She is as tall as I am and very thin. I feel sorry for her because her face is so scarred on one side. Even more than her hair can cover."

My brain slipped into gear.

"Scalded?" I asked.

Sofia didn't seem to hear me.

"I am curious to know how it will feel to be used by a woman. That is not what she wants. She shows me pictures and asks which belong together. Then she tells me to add numbers in my head. More and more numbers. Bigger and bigger. Faster and faster. Until they are too many and too big and too fast for me."

It sounded like an IQ test, but I didn't say anything.

"I think that is strange but the man who owns me tells her he was right and I am too smart for my own good and she should pay the price he is asking and not haggle so much."

"The woman bought you?"

"I think at first she will be cheated. I think the man who owns me will take her money and maybe kidnap her for more. But later I see why he cannot do this. The woman has many men with her. Men with cruel eyes and automatic guns."

"How long have you worked for The Scalded Woman?" I asked.

"How do you know of her?"

"Do you want to go back?" I asked. "To Moldova?"

"The police ask me that. They come and they want me to spy for them and they say when it is done and everyone is in prison then they will give me counselors and after that I can go back to Moldova. It is like I am unclean with some disease and I cannot be among other people until I am cured. I want to spit on the police but I am polite when I say no."

"Do you want to go back on your own terms?"

"To be an animal on a farm?" she asked. "To bring babies for some brute who can write only his name and nothing more?"

"What do you want?"

She put Luther on his back on her lap and began to stroke his tummy. "I want you to not go to Georgia. I want Alexander to not go. You will stop him?"

I wondered how much of her background Falkenberg knew. Probably all of it, if my experience with him was any guide.

"What's going to happen in Georgia?"

She let the question drift, smiling down at Luther and cooing at him in a language I didn't recognize. I took some more of my drink to work up the nerve to ask the next question.

"What do you do for The Scalded Woman?"

"I do as I am told."

"Which is?"

"I am to keep men interested," she said. "Sometimes while price is negotiated. Sometimes for other reasons I am not told."

My mind conjured up images of oily suppliers the Scalded Woman was trying to separate from objets d'art and antiquities; images of jaded sophisticates with bank accounts bloated by corruption looking to buy one more trinket, one more conquest.

She smiled at my discomfort. "I am trained to be still and listen, never to flirt, to treat these men as if they are as important as they think they are and to stay always a step out of reach. Once such men have used a woman, they will despise her and she will be of no value. It must be a woman like me only because the outcome cannot always be controlled. If I am used or hurt, I must not panic and go to the police. It is possible to train someone who will not panic to behave well. It is not possible to train someone who is well behaved not to panic. This is what I am told."

"The training must have been intense. The results are impressive."

"No one will teach you if you do not work to learn."

The price of passage. Moldova to Monte Carlo, and probably a lot of other fancy and not so fancy places. When I first saw her, I thought her greatest asset was her looks. Now I knew it was the grit she had found to parlay them into the best life available to her.

"How do you know of The Scalded Woman?" she asked, putting Luther down.

It was the second time she had asked the same question. That made it important, and gave me a chance to get her talking along lines that might tell me something useful.

"Interpol hauled me in for an interview. They know about the gang's trade in black market antiquities but they think the woman herself is chimera."

She didn't know the word.

"Vapor," I explained. "Hallucination."

"I will show you."

She went to the spare bedroom and came back with a photo album from her luggage, paperback sized, just enough to carry a few treasured snippets along on her travels. We sat together on the sofa and she opened it on the coffee table to a five by seven print. The backdrop was brutal mountain country, bare and craggy and snow capped. Four people stood around the hood of a Land Cruiser looking at something spread out there. Three of them had the look of Afghan thugs from the six o-clock news. Sofia put a manicured fingernail on the fourth.

"Her," she said.

Only careful dress suggested a woman. Jodhpurs tucked into knee high boots and a British military sweater tucked into the jodhpurs. An olive drab balaclava covered all but a bit of her face. The assault rifle slung over her shoulder was an A4 Colt rather than the Ak-47s carried by the others.

"She looks pretty tough," I remarked.

"She is in a man's world," Sofia said. "She is horribly burned and will never be adored. She has only those who work for her. We are her family."

"And she wants the Alexandria Scrolls?" I asked.

"She tells me of them," Sofia said. "She says to each person's life there comes only one crowning achievement."

"And the Scrolls are hers?"

"As you think they are yours."

I hadn't realized I was that transparent. "A lot of people have caught the fever. The first look from the academic world is that they are the real deal. Even if they turn out to be copies of known works, they'll probably be the oldest existing copies. They are worth recovering."

She just shook her head. "You think as a good person thinks. Bad people seek to take the Scrolls from a dangerous place. Many will perish. You should not be among them. Alexander should not."

"That sounds pretty specific," I said. "Can you give me any details?"

"Georgia is not the U.S. I know how it is from Moldova. Evil men do as they wish and then pay the Archbishops to bless away their sins."

She closed the photo album and the subject with it. "Do you have *National Velvet* on DVD?"

The question came out of nowhere and caught me completely by surprise. She had just finished telling me things no woman would ever confess, for reasons I couldn't begin to imagine, and now she was off on a completely random track. If nothing else, the DVD was a way to assuage my guilt for dredging up her past. I went to rent a copy while she unpacked.

The movie was a juvenile horse melodrama. She watched it as raptly as a pre-teen. I wondered how many different Sofias might lurk behind the veneer and the grit.

Next morning I drove her to Shilshole Marina. She wore military boots, cargo pants and a pea coat. No head scarf this trip. Her hair was tucked up under a knit cap. She responded to none of my attempts at conversation and didn't initiate any of her own until we reached the marina parking lot.

"I am not sure if I made a mistake," she said.

"Coming to see me?" I asked.

"Not coming to your bed last night. Not making you use me. After a man has used a woman he is disgusted with all women. That way you would not be so foolish when Barbara Wren comes."

I didn't quite laugh at the idea. "Mrs. Wren has better things to do than visit me."

"She will come."

I pulled into a parking spot and shut down the Honda. There were no good-byes. She just opened the door and got out.

"You must not touch me," was all she said.

Two men were walking toward the car. Their dress was western but they were middle-eastern in cast. They weren't displaying any automatic guns but Sofia had been right about the cruel eyes. I got out and opened the trunk and stood aside.

One man recovered Sofia's luggage. The other watched. Her parting words were a warning.

"I cannot help you if you come to Georgia. No matter what."

She and the two men went down a flight of stairs and threaded the maze of piers. The boat they boarded was a sleek inboard. It rumbled to life, idled out of the Marina and took off up Puget Sound with a glass-rattling roar. The Scalded Woman seemed to have a long reach and a lot of assets. It could be she was marshalling her forces in Georgia to pursue the Scrolls. And that Sofia had been told to detour through Seattle to warn me off. Although I couldn't imagine why anyone would care where a nobody like me went or what I did.

There was one message on the phone recorder when I got home. It was from Barbara Wren.

Chapter 11

The number Barbara left on my machine belonged to an exclusive downtown hotel. An automated switchboard shunted my call-back to her room.

"Owen," she said with just the right touch of charm. "It's nice of you to get in touch so promptly."

She was in Seattle on business, needed to make a side trip to Victoria and was curious to know if I would like to ride up with her on the Clipper.

The Clipper was a high-speed tourist ferry that ran through Puget Sound and across the Canadian border. Barbara and I were the only passengers who boarded without cameras. We staked out a semi-secluded section of railing; a geek in chinos and a windbreaker and an elegant creature in a woolen dress coat. I was more interested in Barbara than in any odd looks we might get.

"So how long have you been in black market antiquities?" I asked.

Sofia had known she would be in Seattle. It wasn't much of a leap to put them in the same business.

"I dislike the phrase 'black market'," was all she had to say.

"How did you get involved?"

That earned me a curious look. Blunt probably wasn't a trait she associated with nervous nerds. I tried not to look as uncomfortable as I felt.

"I met a man," she said, and let a hint of mockery into her eyes. "Isn't that how prim young maidens are lured into lives of sin?"

"It was a serious question." I needed to sort out who the players were and what teams they were on.

The Clipper freed itself from the dock with a lurch that bumped us together. She lingered for a moment longer than necessary. Not enough to qualify as cozying up, just enough to give me a heady dose of fragrance. A float plane lifting out of the city from Lake Union reminded me that any of the local air taxi services could have put her in Victoria in a third of the time the Clipper took. She had invited me to find out whether I was sucker enough to come, and if I was, to work her magic. For what reason I could only wait to learn.

"His name was Christopher Wren," she said, "after the English architect. He was a number of years older; a bachelor who needed an arm ornament for social occasions. For me it was entrée into a world I had only read about. We married eventually but ours was a love born of comfort with each other rather than any consuming passion."

"A middle-aged middle man," I guessed. "Wealthy clients on one end and field people like Eddington on the other."

"Roald worked with Christopher for many years."

All very clubby and British. "Where did that leave you when your husband passed away?"

"I inherited the family business."

"What did Roald and the others think about that?"

"They had ambitions, of course, but ultimately it's about contacts and I was the one who knew the customers."

Her eyes let me know I was approaching treacherous ground. Since my chances with her were the square root of zero, I had nothing to lose.

"Alex Falkenberg among them?" I asked. "Or did you cultivate him on your own?"

"Perhaps you didn't mean that quite the way it sounded?"

"You introduced Eddington to Alex," I pointed out. "Next thing anyone knows, Alex has a new arm ornament."

"And you think Roald conspired against me?"

"Eddington wants to become Christopher in more ways than one," I ventured, expanding on a remark Beatte Czhed had made. "He wouldn't have liked the idea of you keeping company with Alex."

A resigned sigh conceded my conjecture as truth. "I have done everything possible to discourage him."

I doubted that Roald was the only one she'd had to discourage. Considering her late husband's circle of contacts, some of the offers had probably been tempting. The fact that she'd spurned them suggested she was a woman who valued freedom above security. And who would take risks, if the payoff looked right.

"What have you heard from Eddington?" I asked. "I mean since the Russians rescued him?"

"I haven't heard from Roald in two months."

"So you finally discouraged him?"

An uneasy silence fell over her; an ominous reaction from a woman neither uneasy nor silent by nature. The dull vibration of the engines seemed a sinister undercurrent.

"He simply stopped communicating," she said, "although I knew from Alex that he was still active."

"That does sound odd," I said, recalling Eddington's love of conversation.

"Intuition warned me to step back from the situation."

"Is that why Sofia was able to move in on Alex?" I asked.

"Be careful of her," Barbara warned. "She plays the waif very convincingly but she is a professional."

"Then you do know her."

"Among other suppliers, I do business with a middle-eastern firm. Their west coast manager learned that I was distancing myself from Alex and said her organization would like to replace me. She offered a commission if I would introduce their representative."

Barbara cutting contact with Falkenberg and his money and connections on nothing more than intuition didn't sound like the whole story. She didn't give me a chance to ask what else was involved.

"Well," she said, eying me like I might actually have possibilities, "you know everything about me but I know nothing about you."

I kept this version of my life focused on business. It still wasn't flattering. Bean counter with short patience, a hair-splitting disposition and authority issues that torpedoed any hope of a career. I glossed over the series of bottom-rung jobs that culminated in my coat-tail ride to the junior varsity jackpot.

"Not the kind of hero you need to bring you the Alexandria Scrolls," I summarized.

She didn't say anything. She didn't have to. On a scale of one to ten I had just fallen off the chart. She had broken contact with Falkenberg and lost contact with Eddington and now she was being disappointed by everyone's perennial fall-back position, Owen Doran.

"How would you go about moving the Scrolls?" I asked. "I mean, would you sell them piecemeal or keep them bundled for a single large transaction?"

"It would depend on content," she said. "A nineteen hundred year old parchment with fifteen lines of text describing a business transaction was recently recovered in Israel. It is valued at several million dollars. Any one of the Scrolls could match or exceed that. If the translators find a stellar item, say one of the lost tragedies of Sophocles, that piece could go into nine figures on its own strength, as well as lending cachet to the others. Alternatively there are collectors who could take the bidding into nine figures to keep the collection intact."

She was talking hundreds of millions of dollars and watching closely for my reaction. I didn't have one. I didn't object to recovering the Scrolls to share with the world, but stealing for profit was best left to the cream of society. They were the ones who were good at it.

"What exactly do you expect of me?"

"You and Alex are going to Georgia to recover the fifty seven Scrolls on your CD and forty three others, content unknown."

For someone who had distanced herself from Falkenberg she had very precise information. And given that Falkenberg and I were two amateurs chasing a treasure coveted by professional traffickers, she shouldn't have given us much chance of success. Unless she knew something I didn't.

"Assuming visa arrangements can be made," was all I fessed up to.

"Two days, I understand."

The hair stood up on the back of my neck.

"You also understand," I said, "that Alex Falkenberg and his last bunch of cronies sold a software company for more than it was worth, probably way more, and if he gets control of the Scrolls and decides they should go to market, any deal will be biased heavily in his favor."

"I'm not talking to Alex," she said. "I'm talking to you."

The message was clear. If I played my cards right, I might step into his shoes. Maybe she had heard about my giving a copy of the Scrolls to Berryman and thought I could be tempted into betraying Falkenberg over the real thing. We were approaching the Strait of Juan de Fuca, where the wind blew directly off the open ocean. She shivered and moved closer. I knew it wasn't for real but it was still an effort to break the spell.

"Want to go inside and get something warm to drink?" I asked.

She took my arm. "I've been dying to hear about your trip to Georgia. It really was a coup, bringing back copies of fifty seven Scrolls."

She listened raptly to my tale of the monastery and Friar Bones. I rendered it in all the detail I could remember in the hope that something I said might trigger an unusual reaction or telling response. I was kidding myself. She was listening to learn how I perceived the world around me and to determine the best way to manipulate me.

The olde English charm of Victoria arrived too soon. Barbara bid me good-bye at the dock and caught a cab to go see her client. I spent the ferry ride back leaning on the rail and letting the salt wind blow her fragrance out of my head.

At first it seemed like she had shared a great deal of herself with me but on reflection she hadn't told me anything I hadn't guessed already or couldn't have learned from other sources. She had dangled the possibility of both money and dalliance but had made no offer. I was watching the San Juan Islands drift past when it dawned on me that the trip had been a mistake.

According to the newspapers Thai Stick marijuana and China White heroin had come through the Islands in the past. Interpol already suspected that the Falkenberg Foundation was being used to bring the Scrolls onto the black market. Now a Foundation officer had just taken a public ride on a smugglers' route with a woman who was almost certainly known to the police as a dealer. I didn't know whether that was part of Barbara's plan or if she just wasn't aware Interpol might be watching.

Her estimate of two days on the visa was accurate almost to the hour. An express envelope arrived just before noon. My tickets were included. Along with an article Jerry Silver had photocopied from a Virginia newspaper.

Lew Manders and his wife had been outgunned but had given an account of themselves. Neighbors reported several minutes of intense firing. Blood trails indicated more than one of the killers had been hit. Mrs. Manders had been too tough to die right away. She had given the police valuable information. Arrests had been made and more were expected. No details were being released. I wadded the article and missed the wastebasket with it.

The Scrolls seemed to carry a curse, like King Tut's tomb. A bandit attack that nearly killed me on my last trip to the Georgian Republic. A smuggler named Sebastian Eglik beheaded in Turkey. The Manders shot dead in Virginia. Barbara Wren frightened away from Falkenberg by an unknown something or someone. Now I was on my way back into Georgia.

Bon voyage, Owen.

Chapter 12

The flight from Seattle to London was coach. At least the ride was smooth and the recession kept a few seats empty. London to St. Petersburg was a shuddering Ilyushin crammed to the bulkheads. Passengers squabbled with the cabin crew. Howling brats put a manic edge on the cacophony. I cleared Customs glad that I had cancelled the economy hotel reservation Jerry's travel agent booked for me and lined up a room at the Radisson.

St. Petersburg would be my last oasis of civilized comfort before Tblisi. Falkenberg's instructions had come in a cryptic e-mail. I was to stop off on my way to Georgia and talk to the professor who led the original dig at Eddington's site. I had no idea where the University was, let alone how to contact someone on the faculty, so I asked the over-scented woman staffing the concierge desk to put through a call for me.

The Professor's name was Silmenov. As soon as he found out where I was staying his English and his attitude improved. He told me he would meet me for lunch at the Canelle Bar and Grill, just off the lobby, in thirty minutes. I was a dozen time zones out of my element and I needed a long nap to focus. He hung up before I gathered the presence of mind to suggest dinner.

Silmenov was in his sixties now, a portly Slav with a neatly trimmed Vandyke. A shawl-collar cardigan with leather elbow patches served notice to the world that he was an academic. The Canelle probably didn't see many academics. It was a place of shimmering linen and perfectly set silver where impeccably tailored foreigners talked lucrative business. Maybe that was why the Russian Maitre'd installed us at a table where we could look out ornate windows at a wide boulevard.

"It is called Nevsky Prospekt," Silmenov lectured. "During the Terror, Bolshevik hooligans machine-gunned protesting Russians just where we are looking. Innocents fell in their hundreds. Do you see their ghosts?"

All I saw was a street where progress was elbowing out established culture, as it had done since the dawn of civilization.

"No," I said, wondering why the old boy had started the conversation on such a gruesome note.

"Those ghosts are not yet a century old," he said. "And you travel to the Caucasus Mountains confident that you will find ghosts older than recorded history."

"You did some looking yourself," I reminded him.

"When I was younger."

He smiled at memories he didn't share. Too many teeth crowded his small mouth, crammed in any which way. Time and tobacco had shaded them brown. He took out an inlaid silver case and offered me a cigarette, spearing one between his lips when I declined. A waiter arrived and deposited menus without saying a word about no smoking. I had left the protection of Big Brother.

Falkenberg's e-mail had instructed me to interview Silmenov but hadn't provided any specifics. The good professor seemed touchy on the subject of his, now Eddington's, dig site. I decided some prying was in order.

"What were you looking for?" I asked.

"I am told the jigsaw puzzle is a favorite American amusement," he said.

"In some quarters," I allowed.

I owned only one. I had found it wandering through a shop full of old stuff during my college years. It stored in a tin and built out into a Playboy Playmate from 1967.

"We were looking for pieces of the puzzle of human history," he said. "My colleagues and I. Before the regime fell. When there was money for such foolishness."

The waiter cruised by and asked if I needed help with the menu. He and Silmenov were both surprised when I rattled off the piroshky I wanted. I had absorbed a little knowledge of the cuisine along with my limited language skills from the Russian programmers Falkenberg and his high tech cronies had recruited as slave labor under the H1-B visa program. I decided to find out how much substance there was to the tales of corruption they had spun.

"The money is back," I said as soon as the waiter was gone, slipping an envelope partway out of my pocket and giving Silmenov a peek at the Euro notes Frankenberg had told me to pick up.

He let out a disgusted snort flavored by acrid smoke. "Do you think all Russians are for sale? Do you think we are all oligarchs and mafia? That we are greedy fools like your bankers and your Wall Street?"

I put the envelope away. "The money is a fee, Professor. Payment for your time and any inconvenience. It is yours regardless."

"What is it you want to know? Perhaps if you just ask, I will tell you. Did you think of that?"

I wasn't here to argue so I shrugged off his prickly attitude. "Why did you pick the dig site?"

"A sophisticated settlement at an altitude that would support only the most basic subsistence spoke eloquently of knowledge waiting to be uncovered."

The waiter arrived with bread and borscht to start the meal. Silmenov told me about the dig while we ate, speaking with a zeal that stripped away the intervening years. He and a cadre of graduate students augmented by local laborers had scraped down to defensive walls and a huge cistern. Radiocarbon dating from surviving bits of charcoal had returned at 1200 BC. An exploratory trench established layers of previous settlement going back some 4,000 years earlier.

"Back to the inundation that created the Black Sea," I recalled.

An indulgent smile bared his dingy teeth. "Are you one of these chaps who believe that was the source of the Biblical story of Noah and the Flood?"

"That wouldn't be as controversial as turning the Hebrews of *Exodus* from lambs of God into thugs for hire," I said to test his reaction to Falkenberg's theory.

"The Bible itself says the Hebrews enjoyed power when they first came to Egypt. In a land and a time when power came only at the point of a spear, what else could they have been but hooligans?"

"Did Professor Eddington ever mention the Alexandria Scrolls?"

"I'm sorry. What?"

The fact that Silmenov asked 'what' rather than 'who' established that Eddington had contacted him. That told me something. If the dig site was just cover for Eddington to hunt the Scrolls, there was no need to talk to Silmenov. Unless Silmenov was meant to be part of the cover.

"Did Eddington ask you to return to the dig site?"

"Eddington?"

The single crisp word followed by sharp scrutiny told me I had hit a nerve. He realized almost as quickly that he had over-reacted. He made too much of lighting a fresh cigarette, snapping the case closed, flashing an engraved lighter, taking the cigarette from between his lips European style with a thumb and forefinger, favoring me with a plume of exhaled smoke. I saw only a quick-witted man uncomfortable with casual pretense.

"Did someone else ask you to return?" I inquired.

He said nothing.

"Maybe to resume your work?"

He crushed out the cigarette, took the last sip of his tea and patted his lips with a napkin.

"Come on, Professor," I said. "That rant about corruption wasn't for my benefit."

"Excuse me? Rant?"

American slang wouldn't help me in Russia. An idea was taking shape out of the fog of jet lag and I needed to articulate clearly to test it.

"You don't care about me. You were lecturing yourself. You turned down an offer you wanted in the worst way. Now you're trying to convince yourself you made the right decision."

He folded the napkin carefully and put it aside. "My decision was correct."

I took out the envelope of Euro notes.

He shook his head. "I would choke on them," he said. "I know that now. I am indebted for that knowledge."

"Why?"

He waved a hand at Nevsky Prospekt outside the elegant windows. "They were also complicit who stood and watched while evil was done in the name of bringing peace and prosperity to Mother Russia."

How urban violence during the Bolshevik terror connected with a remote archeological dig in the Caucasus Mountains, I couldn't fathom.

"Professor, I'd really appreciate your being more specific."

"Go home," he said. "While you still can."

He stood and doddered out of the restaurant. It would be easy to dismiss him as a goofy old man full of trivial secrets. He wasn't. He was a respected academic posted to a premier university who was still being contacted about his earlier work by people and for reasons he wouldn't discuss.

"Go figure," I said to myself.

"Excuse me, sir?" the waiter inquired.

"Nothing."

I asked for the check and spent the wait brooding. Silmenov had never heard of the Scrolls. He shouldn't have anything to worry about beyond hardening arteries and a skinny pension. Instead he was turning down money and muttering in his whiskers about evil done in the name of peace and prosperity for Mother Russia. I couldn't understand why he hadn't taken the opportunity to return to the dig site to finish the work he started in his prime. And I couldn't shake the feeling his secrecy was for reasons both current and ominous. I paid the check and went out to the lobby.

The desk clerk had a telegram for me.

Imperative you take first available flight Tblisi. Check into Courtyard Hotel. Wait there. Falkenberg.

It was the crudest possible fraud. Falkenberg loved to talk but he hated to write. Even if conditions reduced him to using a telegram, it would have read:

Tblisi. FPW. Courtyard. Falk.

I had the concierge put a call through to D.C. Given the time difference, Jerry Silver should have been in bed. Instead he was awake and dithering.

"Where are you? The hotel in St. Petersburg said you cancelled your reservation."

I told him about switching accommodations. "Where is Falkenberg?" I asked.

"He missed this afternoon's conference call."

That didn't sound like Falkenberg. He never missed a chance to run his mouth.

"Have you had any word from him?" I asked.

"I received a telegram. Instructing me to go to Tblisi. I couldn't confirm it."

I told him about my telegram, not having any idea who would want the entire Falkenberg Foundation in the Republic of Georgia, or why. Or how they had found me when Jerry couldn't.

"Have you checked with the American Embassy in Tblisi?" I asked.

"Of course," he snapped.

I began thinking unpleasant thoughts. "Did the police solve the Manders killings?"

"A father and four sons were arrested. Self styled bounty hunters. Someone hired them. If the police know who, they aren't saying. What does that have to do with Alex?"

"I have no clue," I admitted, as much to myself as Jerry.

"Well, find him," Jerry snapped. "You're the one on the ground. Find him."

"I'll do what I can," was all I committed to.

I had the concierge fix me up with a rail connection to Tblisi. The telegram had said fly. I'd take an oxcart before I got on an airplane.

Chapter 13

What sleep I got was on the night train to Kiev. I spent a brief layover trying to walk off the stiffness, my hands thrust in my pockets and my shoulders hunched against the pre-dawn chill. The city was a mix of rococo facades that had stood for centuries and hard-edged Soviet construction that had grown like scar tissue in the wounds of World War II. It was an alien environment, forged during a time I had only read about. Empty streets and foreign signage brought a creeping sense that I was alone and isolated. I went back into the terminal and found my boarding platform.

The 31/38 was billed as the fast train to Tblisi. The trip would take only seven hours. It began with a slow chug through grimy industrial facilities. We picked up speed passing rows of soulless apartment buildings and rattled our way out into the monotony of the Ukraine. Beyond the drizzle running down the window the scenery ranged from dismal to bleak; probably still radioactive from Chernobyl. I shut out the incomprehensible chatter and unfamiliar odor of the other peasants in the car and settled in for some serious brooding.

Setting out for Tblisi full of determination to find Falkenberg was one thing. Actually finding him would be another. I didn't know the city. I didn't know the language. I had no contacts who could help me. If Falkenberg were in real trouble I would be no use at all. In addition to my many other shortcomings I was also a poster boy for cowardice. I even started when someone took the empty seat next to me.

She was in her early twenties. The residue of acne kept a pleasant face from outright beauty. And she was obviously American. No one else would be schlepping around Eastern Europe in tight jeans, a hoodie and a baseball cap with a blonde pony tail sticking out the back.

"Hello," she said in a perky voice.

I returned the greeting and we exchanged names. Hers was Mary Ann. My take on her was recent graduate fulfilling her long-cherished dream of a European tour before she married her stalwart sweetie from State U., had a couple of kids and settled down to the things that really mattered, like clawing her way up the social pecking order. That was fine with me. She was a chance to get my mind off my dilemma, talk to someone who spoke English and reinforce my commitment phobia, all at the same time.

Then she asked, "Did you know that we are living in the End Times?" and blew my theory.

"Missionary?" I asked.

"Have you heard of Dr. Aaron Skinner?" She spoke the name with a reverent hush.

"No."

"Do you have a laptop with you?" she asked. "I have one of his DVDs."

I didn't say anything. I couldn't see wasting battery capacity on some overwrought Bible banger.

That didn't discourage Mary Ann. "I have his book, too."

She rummaged in a shoulder bag and brought out a fifteen dollar-sized trade paperback priced at twenty five. The title was *Christ and the Coming Apocalypse*. The cover featured a stern-faced medieval version of Jesus looking down on smoldering ruins and suffering victims with a mushroom cloud in the background. No doubt about it, folks. Armageddon was nigh.

"No thanks," I said.

"Take it."

I shook my head rather than say something impolite.

She pushed it at me. "Read it. You need to know about the times we're living in. About what the *Book of Revelation* says."

"There are no actual revelations in the *Book of Revelation*," I said. "It was ginned up around 90 AD by some loser doing time on an island off the coast of Turkey."

She stared at me like I had just landed from Mars.

"Don't you watch the History Channel?" I asked.

She unzipped a pocket on my back pack and pushed the book inside. "You have to learn about *Revelation*," she insisted.

"I read the original," I said.

I recalled most of it dimly from Sunday school. Mr. Palmer, who taught us, had been a compact, smiling man who never, ever lost his composure. He had scared me worse than all the baseball coaches who yelled at me for muffing grounders.

"It's not enough," she said. "Do you know the secret of the Seven Seals?"

I didn't know any secrets but the phrase had cropped up in news account of the mess in Waco, when the Feds had shot it out with a sect called the Branch Davidians.

"Dr. Skinner knows," Mary Ann announced. "He is the only one who knows what the Seven Thunders will speak."

"Well, if he's the only one who knows, then he didn't put it in the book, and if he didn't put it in the book, what's the point of reading the book?"

That required thought, and I could see she wasn't comfortable with thinking. She gave me a disappointed look. I wasn't hearing the Word.

"Do you know of the Anti-Christ?" she asked.

That conjured up Hollywood images of dark clouds, ominous music and heavy breathing. "Some sort of preacher, wasn't he?" I asked to see if I could needle Mary Ann about her favorite pastor.

"He's going to read from the Alexandria Scrolls and make people believe he is Jesus," she declared. "He is going to make them worship him as a false god."

My interest in the Scrolls and my itinerary had better circulation than *The Wall Street Journal*. I tried to keep the surprise out of my voice.

"How did you know where to find me?"

"Everything is known," she warned.

That much was obvious. "The question was how."

"You don't need to be afraid. Dr. Skinner has sent his Mighty Men to find the Scrolls."

"What's Skinner going to do with the Scrolls?"

"Destroy them."

"Vandalizing historical treasures will get him locked away for a long time," I said.

"They must be destroyed. To deny the Anti-Christ."

"I don't think the authorities are going to buy that," I said. "They tend to want evidence, not prophecy."

"The Anti-Christ has already risen," she declared. "The Mighty Men slew him as Goliath was slain, and now he has risen."

I would have put the claim down to religious flummery if she didn't look and sound absolutely serious. With Sebastian Eglik and the Manders dead by violence, it seemed worth following up on.

"Do you have any details?" I asked. "Names? Dates? Places?"

She stood and looked down at me with disdain.

"Accept Jesus Christ as your personal savior," she admonished. "Only then can the Mighty Men protect you."

She went off along the aisle and out of the car without a backward look.

If it weren't for a residual aroma of toilet soap I would have dismissed the whole thing as an hallucination born of sleep deprivation. Harmless or not, Mary Ann hadn't come on her own. Someone had sent her. The fact she had found me on a train that I had caught on the spur of the moment meant I was being closely watched. I should have taken Falkenberg's rant about religious kooks and the Scrolls more seriously.

Dr. Skinner's weighty tome seemed like a good place to do some research. Skinner's bio was on the back cover. It painted a glowing picture of scholarly vision and dynamic leadership tempered by a genuine feel for the common man. His photo showed a mane of silver hair and facial lines that put his age around sixty. He stood with one hand upraised and a microphone in the other. In the background, an audience had come to its feet.

I spent the rest of the ride to Tblisi reading that Islamic terror, global warming, AIDS, exploding populations, nuclear proliferation, tsunamis and hurtling asteroids were all manifestations of the Biblical prophecy of the End Times. When I got to the advertising in the back, however, it turned out that I had a little grace to repent. Those who yearned to be shown the way could receive the Guidance Package for twelve easy monthly payments of $124.99. Anyone who was really into rejoicing at the feet of the Lord could score the Salvation Package, a bargain at twenty four monthlies of $249.99. If littering hadn't made me feel guilty, I would have left it on the seat when I disembarked.

Watching to see if anyone followed was an exercise in futility. I was in a foreign country. Everyone looked sinister.

The main exit from the train station emptied out onto a busy sidewalk where the unwary could go over like bowling pins. I hauled my luggage through the pedestrian bustle, detoured around a man pushing a wheelbarrow full of dead geese and climbed into the least appalling cab at the curb, a decrepit diesel Mercedes.

The interior reeked of too many years and too many passengers. Even that wasn't enough to cut the acrid bite of industrial pollution that hung in the air. The driver made his way through a jam of trucks and trams and cars and motorbikes of every description but new and deposited me at the Villa Berika. I watched him chug away in a cloud of blue smoke, chilled by the feeling that I was on my own in a strange city, facing an impossible task and watched by an uncounted number of unsympathetic people.

Based on what little research I had been able to do, the Villa Berika looked like the best bet among Tblisi Hotels. The desk staff had some experience catering to finicky western tourists, although I didn't think I'd take them up on their sole English-language entertainment brochure printed in cooperation with the Diana Casino. I couldn't see myself hopping into a cab and telling the driver to take me to 123 Tsinamdzgvrishvili Street.

I unpacked and had the concierge put through a call to the woman who had been my case officer at the Embassy on my last trip. She wasn't happy to hear I was back but she did verify that the Embassy was looking for Falkenberg and told me to report any information I received. My stomach was growling by then. It had never made peace with unpronounceable ethnic dishes but I was tired of nutrition bars so I decided to try a trip down to the hotel restaurant in the hope that the menu had enough bland stuff to make a full meal.

It was a warm place, dim lit, with an air of European decadence and a buzz of unintelligible conversation from a good-sized dinner crowd. Once I convinced the maitre'd that I was a hotel guest, he condescended to seat me in an out of the way corner. A waiter deigned to leave a menu and I fell to studying it.

"What are you having?"

The voice surprised me. It belonged to Mary Ann the missionary.

Her dress looked like local procurement. The kind of straight-forward, tight-fitting affair a girl needed to maneuver Mr. Right into the kind of situation where daddy would get his shotgun and march them both to the nearest church. Not that Mary Ann would be mistaken for a local. She had graduated from the Sherwin-Williams School of Make-up. She helped herself to the chair across from me.

Chapter 14

"I didn't think we'd be staying at the same hotel," Mary Ann said while she made a production of unfolding her napkin and spreading it on her lap.

I doubted that we were. The Villa Berika was priced for people who threw around money, not sermons. The waiter brought another menu and did his best to render the specials into English. Mary Ann mispronounced the one salad I recognized and ordered a main course I didn't. The soup du jour was corn chowder. I told the waiter I wanted my beef well done.

Foreign food wasn't necessarily dirty but any lingering bacteria would be different strains than American immune systems were used to. I made it a point never to eat anything that hadn't been cooked to the temperature of Hell's hinges. The wine steward showed up touting a five year old claret. For all I knew it was a fifty-fifty mix of ketchup and kerosene they'd stirred up in the basement five minutes ago. I shook my head.

Mary Ann gave me a disappointed look. Whoever sent her probably told her I was an easy mark. Any junior varsity Jezebel could wrap me around her little finger. I should be acting suave. Coming on. Plying her with giggle-water. Fat chance. I wanted her cold sober. I had questions.

"Where is Alex Falkenberg?" I asked.

Her smile vanished and her voice fell to a warning hush. "He is a disciple of the Anti-Christ."

At least she had heard of him. As short as I was on leads, that alone was good news. Also, if he was just a disciple and not the actual Anti-Christ, he hadn't been slain by any Mighty Men. Although I wasn't sure how seriously to take that part of the fairy tale.

"One thing I don't get," I said. "You believe the Bible is the Word of God, don't you?"

"Yes," she said.

"Absolute truth? Cannot be contradicted?"

"Yes."

"So why is your Doctor Skinner trying to slay the Anti-Christ? If the prophecy in *Revelation* is right, and you and Skinner claim to believe it is, then God is going to chuck the Anti-Christ into a burning lake. Nothing you or Skinner can do will change the outcome."

"You don't understand."

"So explain it to me."

"I can't."

"Why not?"

"Only Doctor Skinner knows the secret of the Seven Seals."

"And the world isn't ready for that," I recalled from his book.

"God appeared to him in a vision and told him what the Seven Thunders will speak."

"Is that what set off whatever you people are doing?"

Her smile was smug. She was on a mission from the great man himself. Nothing could shake her secrets loose. My chowder and her salad arrived. She didn't raise an eyebrow when I soaked my bread in the steaming liquid to do away with any microscopic creepy crawlies. Her own style of eating reminded me of school cafeterias and summer camps. Probably religious camps in her case.

"So how did you come to join Dr. Skinner's flock?" I asked.

She gave me a starry-eyed summary. Her mother had attached them to a succession of Evangelical groups while she was growing up. The last was Skinner's. Mary Ann told me about attending a big rally with her mother, meeting the parson in person and going to missionary training.

"So," I asked again, "how did you go from spreading the gospel to stalking the Anti-Christ?"

"You're mocking me."

She was miffed. I wasn't having much luck probing for what, if anything, she knew about Falkenberg and his whereabouts. I had to put the drugstore psychology on hold when the waiter arrived with our entrees.

I never would understand chefs. They took a perfectly good piece of meat, sliced it into flawless medallions that cooked through evenly to bring out every drop of flavor and then sauced it up to taste like a combination of garlic and orange rinds. And just in case their masterful creation reached some Philistine like me who didn't savor their efforts, the waiter put out an assortment of bottled sauces to smother everything. Not much different, I supposed, from Mary Ann hiding behind the tight dress, the make-up and the Bible-banging.

"Okay," I said. "The least I can do in common politeness is ask who the Anti-Christ is. I mean, what name is he using to walk among us and preach evil?"

"Roald Eddington."

I almost choked on a medallion of beef. Eddington might be a little light in the scruples department but at fifty odd years and three hundred pounds, I couldn't picture him with fire in his eyes and steam boiling out of his ears.

"How exactly did you, or Doctor Skinner, identify Eddington as the Anti-Christ?" I didn't recall him sporting any 666 tattoos.

"I told you," she said. "He was slain as Goliath was slain. And now he has risen."

An idea began to percolate. "There may be a little confusion here. Eddington wasn't slain. He was kidnapped. By Chechen bandits."

"He was slain. By the Mighty Men. He has risen."

"He was rescued by Russian commandos."

She shook her head vehemently. "He was slain as Goliath was slain. He has risen."

She obviously didn't want to let go of the idea. I needed to shake her conviction if I was going to get any useful information out of her.

"If that's true, how will you ever get off square one?" I asked.

She stared at me.

"I mean, look at the situation logically. The Mighty Men slay the Anti-Christ. The Anti-Christ rises from the dead. Suppose you get lucky and track him down again. The Mighty Men slay him again. What's to stop him from rising from the dead again? You're in a never-ending loop here."

"Only God can slay the Anti-Christ," she declared. "You said so yourself. Not even Jesus or the Angels. God will cast the Evil One into a lake of Fire and Brimstone. It's all in *Revelation*."

"Okay. Fine. We're in agreement. So why are you people chasing Eddington if he really is the Anti-Christ and you can't do anything about him?"

"Doctor Skinner is going to find the Alexandria Scrolls. He's going to destroy them so they can't be used against Jesus."

The only religious person I ever believed in was Luca Paccioli, the Italian Friar who invented double entry book-keeping. After reviewing Doctor Skinner's price list, I wasn't buying into the idea that he would destroy anything as valuable as the Alexandria Scrolls. More likely he'd throw a load of counterfeits into a public bonfire and sell the real items into the black market. Trying to convince Mary Ann of that would be an exercise in frustration.

"Okay," I said, "back to the original question. Where is Alex Falkenberg?"

"The Mighty Men will find him."

I didn't know if that was a threat or a promise but it did mean that Skinner's crowd didn't know where Falkenberg was either. It also ended any hope of Mary Ann adding value to my quest. We were the only two Americans in a restaurant full of East European babble, so I was stuck listening to her religious chirping. As soon as we finished the main course, I asked for the check.

Mary Ann wasn't going to be put off that easily. She rode up in the elevator with me and walked along to my door. I was getting tired of every woman I met thinking she could play me for a sucker. Never mind that they were almost always right.

"Where are you really staying?" I asked, just in case I did have to get in touch.

"Do you have a guest bar in your room?" she asked.

"That's not an answer."

She gave me a fetching smile. "I'd like a glass of wine."

There was no point in trying to get her drunk. She wasn't the type anyone trusted with important information. And she had already given me my next step when she mentioned Eddington. He probably made a beeline for Tblisi as soon as he got out of the hospital in St. Petersburg to go after the Scrolls. And he was the first person Falkenberg would have contacted. If Eddington didn't know where Falkenberg was, he at least had some local contacts and a rudimentary grasp of the language so he could help me look. I needed to lose this chick so I could contact the concierge and get a call through to the British Embassy to locate him.

Normally getting women to avoid a nerd like me was a slam dunk. But when all else failed, there was one sure way to send them packing. I opened the door, let Mary Ann in and closed it behind us. Night had fallen outside. City lights cast their glow through the window and made long shadows in the room.

"Where's the light switch?" she asked.

"Who needs it?"

I put my arms around her, one hand on her bottom and the other at the nape of her neck and pushed my mouth against hers. Surprise had her mouth open and I took advantage of the situation to stick my tongue in. She squirmed furiously. I released her.

"What's the matter," I asked. "Isn't this what you came for?"

"No!"

She was panting in the dimness. I could feel the warmth on my face. It occurred to me that I had her backed against a wall. The idea was to scare her off. Not get my own temperature up. I stepped away to cool off.

"Do you want to take it slower?"

"No!"

She got her breath back and composed her voice.

"I mean, um, turn on the lights."

"Okay, I'll tell you what. I'm a bit pressed for time right now. Why don't you go find your Anti-Christ and I'll go find Alex Falkenberg and we'll meet back here afterward and give it another try."

"No," she blurted.

"Okay, then, we'll just forget it."

"You can't leave."

"Why not?"

"You just can't. That's all."

"We're both leaving," I said. "Even if I have to call the management and have you removed."

"Wait. Can't we talk?"

"No."

"Just for a minute."

"No."

I moved to open the door. I never made it. She threw her arms around my neck and kissed me hard.

Chapter 15

Biology ran roughshod over my common sense. Getting Mary Ann's dress off without snagging the zipper was a small miracle. Beyond that it was all fumbling. Her squirming and squealing and giggling ratcheted up my excitement. I maneuvered her onto the bed. She was active underneath me. I didn't know whether she was responding, resisting or just trying to hurry me along to get it over with. I lay on my back afterward, listening to my own ragged breathing.

The bedside lamp came on and made me squint. Mary Ann rummaged among the bed clothes, demanding to know what I had done with her underwear. She found it, retrieved her dress from the floor and retreated into the bathroom. A residue of cloying perfume hung over me like trench gas. I rolled off the bed and came unsteadily to my feet.

Unfamiliar exercise and travel kinks left me with the coordination of Frankenstein. Not that there was any hurry. Growing up with two sisters had taught me it would be a while before the bathroom door opened. I applied a booster shot of deodorant and put on fresh clothes for my trip down to the concierge.

Mary Ann came out dressed and made up. "I'll be leaving now," she announced.

She made it very clear, just in case I had become smitten and possessive. I stepped to the door and opened it with a gallant flourish.

A man was waiting just outside. Leather jacket, tight jeans, just the right touch of facial scruff. Bad boy chic. Here it is, girls. Come and get it. I wasn't quick enough to slam the door before he put a motorcycle boot against the jamb.

Mary Ann gave me a reassuring smile. "Don't be afraid. If you embrace Jesus Christ as your personal savior, the Mighty Men will protect you."

"Do you have a name?" I asked the Mighty Man.

"Yeah," was all he said.

Mary Ann was more forthcoming. "This is Rick Judson," she chirped. "Doctor Skinner sent him just because of the Scrolls."

Anything blessed by Doctor Skinner was fine and dandy as far as she was concerned. She probably had been told to get me to my room, keep me there and keep me quiet until Judson could arrive. She had made her sacrifice for Jesus and she had every right to be proud of herself.

Judson jerked his head at me. "Okay, dude, you're coming with us."

He was four inches taller than I was and his fifty pounds weight advantage looked to be all muscle. It was enough to worry me but not enough to move me. There was no way I was being taken to some unknown corner of a foreign city in the middle of the night.

"Get lost," I said, "or I start yelling and bring hotel security and the police down on you."

My threat had more impact than I expected. Judson's eyes lost focus. His jaw slacked. His knees buckled. He fell forward. I had to jump aside to keep from being knocked over.

Judson landed face down on the carpet at my feet and didn't move. A slim, swarthy man took Judson's place in the doorway. The man's windbreaker was water-spotted, his face pock-marked under a snap brim cap, his eyes bright with the edgy sheen of adrenaline. I had never seen a real blackjack but the tightly sewn leather dangling from his hand looked just like the movie version. I didn't move.

Mary Ann started to back-pedal. The man was quick. He hurdled Judson, grabbed Mary Ann around the waist and clamped a hand over her mouth.

She squirmed and kicked.

"Be still," a female voice instructed. "You will not be molested."

I knew the voice.

Without it I might not have recognized Sofia. She was cased neck to ankles in a woolen overcoat with the collar turned up behind a formal black Muslim head scarf. I stepped back to make way for her.

There was no hint of fragrance as she passed. Only facial symmetry and elegant carriage to remind me of the woman I had seen in America. She took Mary Ann's bag and recovered a wallet, passport and a fat pen that looked like camouflage for pepper spray. Everyone seemed to have forgotten I existed. I risked a glance at the door.

A second swarthy man appeared there. Squat and stocky, he filled the doorway from side to side. His face had been battered and scarred in countless fights. A crooked smile told me I wasn't getting past him.

The slim man released Mary Ann. She backed against the wall, silently mouthing the Lord's Prayer. The man went through my pockets and lifted a decoy wallet. When I travelled, paranoia kept my valuables in a belt velcroed around my waist under my clothes.

The next event was a slick bit of teamwork that was over almost before it started. Sofia slapped Mary Ann's face. Mary Ann scuttled sideways out of reach, away from the wall. That exposed the back of her head. The slim man blackjacked her. The squat heavyweight caught her over one shoulder as she fell. A third swarthy man appeared in the hallway, wheeling a laundry hamper. The foot sticking out probably belonged to a back-up Mighty Man. The squat heavyweight dumped Mary Ann in. I gave them room to man-handle Judson's limp weight.

"You must come with us," Sofia informed me.

A door opened across the hall and one of my neighbors poked a balding head out to check on the rumpus. Sofia stepped into the hallway, looking every inch the Muslim aristocrat. The kind of woman who wouldn't be allowed out of the house without a protective entourage of cut-throats. The kind of men who might make a fatal event out of a sideways glance. My neighbor shut the door.

"Come quietly," Sofia ordered, and her posse positioned themselves to make sure I obeyed.

This wasn't the Sofia who had sat on my couch stroking Luther the cat and telling me her life story. This was the Sofia who had spent endless, bitter nights on the street waiting for men to come and pay to use her. She led the way along the hall to a freight elevator and pressed the call button. The automatic she slipped out of her coat pocket was all business; worn blue steel with a grip that fit her hand perfectly, a familiar and preferred travelling companion. She held it down at her side. I had the uneasy feeling that any people aboard when the elevator door opened were toast.

The car was empty and we rode down to re-enact the drama at the bottom. The door opened on a basement alcove, poorly lit and deserted. Sofia's crew pushed the laundry hamper out. A service door opened onto a loading dock. The drizzle had grown into a relentless rain that all but emptied the nearby street. Three vehicles idled at the curb. Soviet era leftovers and worn out German miscellany weren't good enough for this crowd. They had brought their own Toyotas. I was installed in the rear seat of a Corolla, next to a rangy man with a Kalashnikov on his lap. Sofia sat in front and retrieved a Colt assault rifle from the floor. The rest of the gang got into two pickups and we pulled out, one truck in front of the sedan, one in back. If heavily armed thugs had to travel in convoy, either the city or the situation, or maybe both, were a lot more dangerous than I had anticipated.

The trip to the car had left me sodden. Cold water dribbled out of my hair and down my face and neck and made me miserable as well as scared. Rain blurred the windows and slowed traffic to a horn-honking crawl. We did a lot of weaving past trucks and busses, which probably meant we were passing through downtown. Nobody said anything. Normally I was comfortable with silence, but my nerves were fraying fast.

"You made good time from Seattle," I told Sofia, mostly to find out if panic had paralyzed my vocal chords as effectively as it had my thinking.

If she was paying attention she didn't show it.

"What was it after the speed boat to Vancouver?" I asked, trying out my best guess and discovering how hard it was to sound suave when my sinuses were congested. "Flight to Vladivostok? Connections to Tblisi?"

"You should have stayed in Seattle," she said.

She sounded concerned that I hadn't. I tried not to read anything personal into it. She had been trained to make men feel like she cared one way or the other. It probably had become habitual.

"Alexander should have stayed in San Francisco," she added.

"Is this how you grabbed him?"

"He was gone when we came to his hotel," she said. "No one has seen him. We look. The American Embassy looks. Everyone looks. But no one has seen him."

That sent a chill up my spine.

The convoy began to make speed. We appeared to be on a boulevard heading out into an upscale suburb. There were a few street lights and they showed walled villas on either side. We left the boulevard and after a minute the lead truck stopped with its headlights shining on a solid metal gate. All the vehicle lights went out and plunged us into darkness. After a minute the convoy crawled forward and we stopped again. Someone opened my door.

"Get out slowly," Sofia instructed. "Make no sudden movements."

The rain came down in sheets and soaked me while I stood beside the sedan. My eyes began to adjust. I could make out that we were in some sort of courtyard. The walls were maybe seven feet tall. A running jump and a good jolt of adrenaline might have put me over but I was wet to the skin, demoralized and surrounded.

"Come," Sofia instructed.

The house was angular and imposing. A massive door opened to reveal a pleasant man in a stylish western suit. Not being a subscriber to *Gentleman's Quarterly* I couldn't be sure, but I doubted that the AK-47 had replaced the shoulder bag as a fashion accessory.

The entry was floored in marble, dimly lit, two stories high. Sofia led me up a curving staircase, knocked on a door at the top and let me into a large room.

There was a fire burning, probably in lieu of the central heating the Georgian Republic was notorious for not having. It was the only light and it sent shadows flickering over ornate furniture and hanging wall tapestries. Before the fire a woman sat in a plush gondola chair. She wore a full length robe and had her bare feet propped on an ottoman. She didn't look up from the computer on her lap.

"Do come in, Mr. Doran," she said in husky English that suggested a British rather than American education. "Sit down. Please."

Chapter 16

Heat from the fire dissipated a few feet from the hearth and left the rest of the room dank. Sofia moved her eyes to indicate an upright wooden chair in the center of the floor. It looked like a lonely and not very comfortable place. I squished across the hardwood in my soggy shoes and sat down shivering.

Sofia closed the door and sat on a divan with the assault rifle on her lap. The only other life in the room was a gray cat. It uncoiled itself from the hearth, yawned while it stretched, and then padded over to where Sofia sat. She moved the rifle from her lap. The cat hopped up and draped itself out. She began stroking it, making a point of not disturbing the woman at the fire. I followed her example and kept my mouth shut.

Beside the woman's chair stood polished cavalry boots. Next to the boots, neatly folded outer clothing lay on top of an armored vest and on top of that lay a Colt assault rifle. She set the computer aside on a small table. Her eyes were dark, closely flanking a hooked, Semitic nose. They caught me looking at the scarred and twisted skin where her straight black hair didn't quite cover the hollow of one cheek.

"You know who I am," she decided.

Cold water dribbled down my face. It was an effort not to fidget.

"I know your reputation with Interpol."

"And what did they say?"

"What you want them to say. That The Scalded Woman is legend. That an organization functions under your pseudonym but that you personally do not exist."

Before she could turn her skeptical expression into words there was a knock and the door opened. The fashion statement with the AK-47 brought in a tea tray. He whispered something to the woman and set a small radio with a short, rubberized antenna on the table. Inspector Nordheim had mentioned Iran in connection with the gang so the low-pitched traffic might have been in Farsi. I didn't understand it any more than I understood why I had been brought here.

The combination butler and rifleman made his way around the room offering delicate, steaming china cups. Apparently even kidnap victims were entitled to basic hospitality. The tea smelled like spinach and tasted worse but at least the cup warmed my hands. The butler waited for a nod from The Scalded Woman before he left.

"Why did you come to Tblisi?" she asked me in a displeased voice that eliminated her as the source of the telegram instructing me to get here pronto.

"I'm trying to find Alex Falkenberg," I said.

Her silence demanded more.

"He missed a conference call," I said. "He never does that."

"Why did Mr. Falkenberg come?" she asked.

It wouldn't help Falkenberg, wherever he was, to tell her he was trying to beat her to the Scrolls. I remembered Eddington's e-mail.

"The Foundation is trying to recover fragments of the Alexandria Scrolls for examination."

"Examination?" Her tone was acid.

"Radio-carbon dating," I said. "Laser refraction to establish the ink composition. That sort of thing."

"Such tests I prefer to arrange myself," she informed me. "German laboratories provide the sort of detailed documentation my more discriminating clients insist upon."

"Did you tell Falkenberg that?" I asked.

"We looked for him only briefly. After someone has gone missing in Georgia for a certain length of time, the probability of live recovery becomes vanishingly small. For practical purposes, Mr. Doran, you are now the Falkenberg Foundation."

My shivering returned in earnest. I had never really entertained the idea Falkenberg could be gone for good. Not that I was much better off myself.

"What do you expect of the Foundation?" I asked.

"What I have always expected. That the Foundation would arrange for an academically sound translation of the Scrolls as a basis for valuation and sale."

"The actual Scrolls," I said, "are, as far as I know, closely guarded in a remote monastery."

"Are you one of these stupid American tourists who see monastics as isolated buffoons living a subsistence lifestyle to prove some pathetic devotion? They are members of a religious network sufficiently vast that neither you nor I could begin to comprehend its reach or its implications."

"I am not a tourist, Madam. I am an accountant. It is in the nature of my training to try to understand the elements of any transaction."

"Do not concern yourself with transactions, Mr. Doran. Try to comprehend the basic truth of your surroundings."

"I have no idea where I am or why I am here, if that's what you mean."

"It is not," she snapped. "Are you incapable of broadening your thinking?"

"I could use some help," I admitted.

"The armor that protects this villa," she said, "came from no factory. It was built to suit in a street-front blacksmith shop. Every sheet and bar and fastener was beaten out by hand. The required strength of the hinges was reckoned solely upon experience. I know this not because I was here when the house was built, but because we are in what Western hubris refers to as the third world and that is the way here. Life is molded by the skill of craftsmen, not by the turn of machines. Denigrate it if you wish, but you cannot deny that it has lasted longer than any technological superpower."

I had no idea what she was rambling about but it gave me an eerie sense of déjà-vu. It was the sort of tangent Falkenberg would go off on just before he dropped some daunting news.

"Mr. Doran, you need to appreciate that you are no longer in a world where you can simply enslave yourself to a single, vast technocracy and be granted comfort and security in return. You have come, against sound advice, to a place where--"

She broke off to listen to a snatch of radio traffic.

"--to a world," she corrected, "where powerful factions struggle for hegemony and individuals, yourself included, must compromise all they hold dear simply to survive."

"Madam, I was brought to this house at gunpoint after watching first-hand the struggle between factions. I get that part of the picture."

She gave her head a hopeless shake. "If you see anything, it is only by the dimmest of light and in the haziest of focus."

The radio interrupted again. She said something curt into the mouthpiece and didn't look happy with the response. She leveled her gaze at me.

"Time is short. I need to know immediately the order of battle, current disposition and operational schedule of Spetnatz."

I was familiar with the word Spetnatz only as some form of Russian special military force. All I had to offer The Scalded Woman was a blank stare.

"Do not trifle with me, Mr. Doran. Major Gregoriev is in field command of Spetnatz forces operating in the Georgian Republic. You went into the mountains with him. You visited their camp."

I remembered Gregoriev only as Eddington's hulking driver. I had no idea he commanded Russian Special Forces operating in Georgia. As far as I knew the Russians had pulled out after their last military adventure and left a few international monitors in their place. The news that they were using Eddington's dig site as a camp made me realize I should have taken Professor Silmenov a lot more seriously.

"Come, come, Mr. Doran. I know the general plan. I need to become familiar with the composition and disposition of forces. More importantly, I need to know Gregoriev's precise schedule. When does he plan to put the operation into motion?"

"I don't know," I blurted. I was still getting used to the idea that Friar Bones had suckered me into carrying a copy of the Scrolls out for translation. Now it looked like I had blundered into something a lot bigger and nastier than black market antiquities. "I've heard nothing about any operation."

"Mr. Doran, I did not put my associates to the risk and trouble of bringing you here without reason. This information is critical. I must have it to finalize my own schedule. And I must have it now."

Her eyes were a warning that the witty repartee was over. I had the feeling my chances of getting out that room alive had just evaporated like the thin smoke from the fire.

"Madam, I assure you, I do not--"

There was a sharp hiss across the room. The cat on Sofia's lap arched to a standing position. The hair on its back stood straight up. It jumped down and streaked across the floor.

Sofia came to her feet, rifle in hand.

The Scalded Woman's radio went nuts. She stood and shucked her robe. She was as tall as I was, thinner and harder. She wore only black briefs. Whatever had scalded her had really done a job. She was scar tissue down her entire left side, from her arm all the way around to her breast and down her abdomen and leg. She slipped into the jodhpurs and pulled on the cavalry boots, pausing only to snap a few words into the radio. A military jacket and balaclava rounded out her ensemble. The armored vest doubled her bulk but didn't seem to weigh her down. She handled the Colt like she knew how to use it. I sat frozen by confusion and uncertainty.

Thunder filled the room. Violent impact jerked the chair out from under me and brought me in for a one point landing. The same impact jolted burning logs out of the fireplace. One rolled idly across the hardwood. It stopped against the wall. Flames licked up and turned the tapestry into a curtain of fire.

Chapter 17

The room began to disintegrate. A crack traced its way down one wall. The crack widened and spider-webbed. A piece of the wall fell away and then the whole wall crumbled and vanished. Wind drove in rain. Burning tapestry billowed, bringing shadowy hobgoblins to life and sending them dancing on swirls of smoke. I got my legs under me and lunged to my feet.

Getting up was one thing. Staying up was another. The room started spinning and I went straight back down. The fall left me on my tail, staring out into the night. A tree had caught fire. Guttering flames showed the villa's iron gate dangling from twisted hinges. Dark figures advanced toward the opening. The Scalded Woman put the laser sight of her Colt on the leader. I heard the report only dimly through the ringing in my ears.

The man dropped in his tracks. Sofia dropped to one knee, braced a foot behind her and launched something that resembled a baseball through the open wall. It arced over the courtyard below and dropped among the advancing figures. I had never seen a real grenade explode before. The flash was dull, almost inconsequential. Men turned to rag dolls and dropped in the street. Flickers of red appeared in the darkness. Incoming gunfire tattooed the walls. Panic boiled up my esophagus and turned my saliva to acid. I flattened on my stomach.

The Scalded Woman was talking a mile a minute into her radio. Sofia traded automatic rifle fire with the people outside. Neither paid any more attention to me than they did to the cat. The hallway door had blown open and the animal scooted out. I wriggled out after it.

The passage beyond was lit only by the jittery glow of flames reflected from the walls. I came unsteadily to my feet. A bullet popped through the wall next to me, throwing plaster into my face. I dropped flat. More bullets came through the wall. I was at the wrong end of a shooting gallery. I used my elbows and knees to propel myself along on my stomach.

Darkness closed around me as I left the burning room behind. My first collision felt like the spindly legs of a table. Something fell and shattered on my back. Judging from the water soaking into my clothes, it was probably a flower vase. My head banged against a wall. I had reached a corner. Smoke began to bother me. I felt a door frame and pawed upward for the handle.

The door opened into a room of uncertain dimensions. Bits of light jittered where wind whipped the drapery away from a broken window. The room looked empty. I tried to come to my feet and charge the window at the same time. A wave of effervescence threatened to lift my head off my shoulders. I stabilized to the point where I could shuffle over and pull the flapping drapes out of my face. Outside I saw nothing but night and rain. I opened the window and scrambled out to let myself down.

It was still a drop from the second floor. Spiny shrubbery broke my fall. It was a struggle to disentangle myself. The world looked less cockeyed after I straightened my glasses. I was in a dim, deserted yard. All the shooting was on the other side of the villa. Only a seven foot wall stood between me and freedom. Elation sent me sprinting and adrenaline gave me the strength to pull myself up.

The crack of a passing rifle bullet penetrated the reverberation in my ears. There was a rifleman on the roof behind me. No amount of lightning fast reaction could have saved me but I had clumsiness on my side. I lost my footing and fell over the far side of the wall before the rifleman could line up a second shot.

The attackers had a machine gun trained on the rear of the villa. Bullets stitched the wall as I flailed down. The gunner probably would have killed me on landing if I hadn't come down flat on my back in the cover of a ditch. I lay in the mud and the pelting rain with the wind knocked out of me, waiting for someone to come and murder me.

Nobody came.

The machine-gunner and the rifleman appeared to be shooting it out. It was a cat and mouse game. A round here and a burst there. The gunfire at the front of the villa had abated to sporadic bursts. I put my head up just high enough to clear the brink of the ditch so I could look for a way out of my predicament.

Two streets made a T-intersection where I lay. One ran past the villa. The other came toward it, but ended at the wall I had gone over. Fire light from the burning villa showed some kind of small truck advancing slowly toward me. Men flanked it on both sides. I wiped my glasses on my sleeve and put them back on.

Mounted on the back of the truck was the slender tube of a recoilless anti-tank cannon. The plan wasn't difficult to figure out. The attackers hadn't had any luck getting through the main gate, so they were going to make their own entrance around back. Right above where I lay. The vehicle stopped. Visions of war movies flashed through my mind. I put my head back down in the ditch, covered my ears and opened my mouth.

The cannon's back-blast lit the night. The impact of the shell was instantaneous. The explosion shook the ground. Pressure crushed against my chest. After that the world was foggy and none too stable. A section had vanished from the wall above. I lay there wondering why the men flanking the cannon weren't charging over me to get into the compound. A surge of shooting erupted from the front gate of the Villa. I risked a look.

A pick-up truck accelerated out of the compound. The bed was full of men firing in every direction. Clouds rose and swirled in the street around them. The defenders had waited until whoever was attacking the villa thinned their forces for an assault on the rear and then thrown smoke grenades to cover a getaway. The men flanking the cannon ran that way in a hopeless effort to head off the escape. Their truck careened after them. Thickening haze made shadows of two sedans leaking automatic gunfire from the passenger windows. Wind brought the smoke my way, obscuring the world from me and me from the world. My eyes told me at least some of it was tear gas. It forced me to my feet and drove me along the street at a wobbly run. Phlegm clogged my throat and started me coughing. I ran until my lungs were on fire and then I pushed myself to walk.

Once the gas was behind me, the effects faded. Emergency vehicle strobes flashed past just one street over but the klaxons sounded miles off. The houses I passed were walled and dark; shut up against the terrors of night. I was alone, coming down from my adrenaline jag, plodding along in a scourging rain, isolated in a foreign city, no idea where I was.

The closest thing to emotion that I could muster was a pervasive sense of inadequacy. My brilliant plan to sneak into Tblisi was compromised before I left St. Petersburg. Gangs of kidnappers descended within hours of my arrival. When real trouble came, all I could do was bail out. My quest to find Falkenberg had turned into headlong flight. I just wasn't up to the job. I was a four-eyed bean counter and I would never be anything else.

A lighted boulevard was visible in the distance. Traffic went by as I approached. I stopped outside a building with a bit of neon over the door and musical cacophony coming from inside. Most likely the Georgian Republic's idea of a night club. A taxi pulled up and a couple got out. They were about my age. Their leather coats and fishermen's caps were probably the latest thing in local fashion. I reached the cab in time to stop the man from closing the door. Whatever he saw in my eyes scared him enough to make him jump back. I shut myself in the rear of the taxi.

"Vi-Villa B-Berik-ka," I stammered at the driver.

He started chattering as soon as we were underway. At least I could hear snatches of what he was saying.

"Yanepanemayou," was as close as I could get to Russian for 'I don't understand'.

The Georgian Republic, I had been told, provided Russia with the same kind of cheap labor Latin America provided the U.S. The language was fairly widely understood here, at least on a rudimentary level. The driver proceeded to demonstrate how rudimentary. We went several blocks before I realized he was describing the nice girl I could meet if I played my cards right.

I cut him off with a quick, "Nyet!" I had already met enough girls for one night.

I pushed some currency at him when we reached the hotel. He gave me a toothy smile, so it was probably too much. The hour wasn't particularly late. People stared when I squished through the lobby. Up in my room I slumped into a chair, glad to be alive. The euphoria faded as aches and pains began to assert themselves. I made my way into the bathroom.

The mirror reflected eyes red from tear gas and hair drying into junior high school cowlicks. Peeling off my wet clothing was no easy task. There were fewer bruises than I expected. That didn't change the fact that I could have been killed. Or that I could still be killed any time anyone took a notion. I showered and sat in my pajamas to brood over my situation.

Going to the police was out of the question. They had interrogated me not two weeks ago over the shooting in the Caucasus. Now I was mixed up in another. Never mind that I was an innocent kidnap victim. I had been in a villa full of career criminals. For all I knew, law enforcement had launched the assault. And all I knew wasn't much. Smugglers and gun-toting evangelicals were chasing the Alexandria Scrolls. Eddington's rescue by commandos, remarks by Professor Silmenov in St. Petersburg and questions from The Scalded Woman suggested some official and unsavory Russian involvement in whatever was going on. Common sense told me to get out of Georgia. My conscience wasn't buying it.

I still had two leads to Falkenberg's possible whereabouts. Eddington and the Monastery where the Scrolls were housed. Falkenberg would have made tracks for one or the other as soon as he was on the ground in Georgia. With luck I might be able to cover both tomorrow and get out of Dodge before sundown. I crawled into bed.

Nightmares came, full of desperate flight, disorientation and shadowy pursuit.

Chapter 18

It was the maid who woke me the next morning. At least she was the one backing out the door making apologetic noises when my eyes popped open. Sunlight through the curtains told me part of the day I had allotted to finding Falkenberg was already gone. I rolled to a sitting position and fumbled the phone off its cradle.

The operator sounded far off and tinny through the residual buzz from last night's explosions. I gave her two phone numbers in succession without connecting. It was after business hours in Washington D.C. Jerry Silver should have answered either his home or his cell. Panic fired my imagination. I saw Jerry gone and me the only one left alive. I had her try his office number and sweated while it rang.

"Catherine Morse speaking." There was television noise in the background so the call had probably auto-forwarded to her home.

"Catherine, this is Owen Doran. I need to speak to Jerry. Can you give me a number where I can reach him?"

"Mister Silver is unavailable." Her emphasis was on the word 'Mister'.

"Has he heard from Alex Falkenberg?"

"Mister Falkenberg is out of the country."

Since strangling her wasn't an option I kept my voice pleasant. "May I leave a message with you, then, please?"

I kept it simple. I would try to locate Falkenberg through Eddington. If that failed, I would try the monastery. If Falkenberg re-established contact, he should return to the U.S. immediately. She read it back to me in a voice that dressed me down for daring to tell a man of Falkenberg's standing what to do. I thanked her and had a call put through to the British Embassy.

My status as Chief Financial Officer of the Falkenberg Foundation got me the name of the hostel where Eddington was staying. If I missed him I didn't want to waste time changing clothes, so I dressed for a trip to the Monastery; long underwear, steel-toed boots, parka. My stomach had too many butterflies to hold down breakfast so I just got into a cab and gave the driver the address of Eddington's lodgings.

The hostel was in a part of the city where buildings shared walls and Soviet era industrial grime had long since smothered any old world charm. It didn't strike me as Eddington's kind of place. It definitely spooked the cab driver. He was gone in a cloud of blue exhaust as soon as he collected his fare. I went into a narrow lobby made smaller by dreary parlor furniture and rang the bell on an unattended desk.

The woman who came was a matronly soul, patient with my halting Russian. Eddington was registered but he hadn't been in for two days. Her face was blank when I described Falkenberg but she did remember that Eddington had left a message for someone. Her husband would know who. She went to hunt him up. I should have been suspicious of anything remotely hopeful. It was Gregoriev who strode into the parlor. His grin was broad and amiable. He caught my hand in his paw before I could make a run for it.

"Ahh, Mr. Doran, the Professor was hoping you would come," he said and clapped an arm around my shoulders. "He is waiting for you."

He was still playing the role of Eddington's driver. Maybe he didn't know that I knew he was a Russian military officer. Maybe he just wasn't taking any chances. He was a lot stronger and better balanced than I was and we were out the door before I knew it. The Land Cruiser was idling at the curb. Gregoriev opened the passenger door.

I managed a smile. "Do you suppose we could stop at my hotel on the way?"

"It will not take long?"

"Hardly any time at all." Just long enough for me to run inside and scream for help.

"Then we stop," he agreed.

It seemed like a better bet than getting shot making a run for it now, so I got in.

I didn't know my way around Tblisi but the route Gregoriev took wasn't the way the taxi had brought me to the hostel. By the time we reached the main highway heading toward the mountains the situation was clear.

"Well, Major," I said, "I guess we won't be stopping at my hotel then?"

"Do not bother with the door handle, Mr. Doran. I took the precaution of disabling it."

Gregoriev let out a booming laugh when it wiggled ineffectually in my hand. Just as abruptly he was dead serious.

"You killed two of my men on your last trip. If you want to kill me, you are welcome to try."

"They shot at me, Major. I shot back." I didn't mention that I was still having nightmares.

"You had a gun with you."

"An old Luger. Bought as a souvenir."

"And now you come to the safe house in Tblisi."

Gregoriev had probably been hiding there. I had just walked in and announced myself.

"How did you find the location?" he asked.

"Eddington registered it with the British Embassy as his residence in the city."

Gregoriev emitted a few guttural syllables. I wasn't up on Russian profanity but he clearly wasn't happy with the good professor.

That got me wondering how Eddington fit into the picture. When I first met him he was an academic gas bag who took me to a monastery where I bought a digital copy of the Alexandria Scrolls. Later he turned out to be an admirer of Barbara Wren, then a suspect in the murder of a black market antiquities dealer named Sebastian Eglik and now he was connected with Russian Special Forces. It seemed likely that his kidnapping by Chechen bandits and supposed rescue by Russian Commandos was a charade, but I couldn't begin to fathom its purpose.

"What are you up to, Major? Doing a little evil in the name of Mother Russia?"

His eyes slitted. "How much do you know?"

"Well, I had lunch with a Professor Silmenov in St. Petersburg."

The name didn't seem to register. In a way that made sense. If the Russian military wanted to re-open Silmenov's dig site, he would have been approached by someone on his own cerebral level. I read Gregoriev as a boots-on-the-ground, get-it-done nasty.

"And I was having tea with the girls from Iran when your thugs crashed the party," I added.

Given the military hardware involved in the attack, and the fact that Gregoriev was in town, it was a good bet he was behind it.

"I did not ask who you had spoken to," he said. "I asked what you knew."

"Beyond the fact that something is about to happen, nothing. However, I may be the only person in the Georgian Republic who doesn't know."

"The Iranian woman. The smuggler. What does she know?"

"Everything but your schedule."

"This is the truth?" he demanded.

From the urgency in his voice I guessed that she was still out there and still a threat. "If she didn't know your plans, how would she know to ask about your schedule?"

"You are doing business with her?" he asked.

"No," I said.

"These pathetic Scrolls? That is your business with her?"

"No."

His hands knotted into fists on the wheel. I wasn't sure whether he wanted to strangle me or The Scalded Woman. Probably both of us.

"Not that I blame you for thinking that," I added quickly. "Several people have accused me of fronting the black market. In fact Interpol has their eye on me for that very thing."

It wasn't much of a threat to begin with, and I was wasting it. Gregoriev wasn't afraid of Interpol. He was hard core military. He probably ate Interpol agents for lunch when the ration truck didn't turn up on time. We had left the city and were rolling through sparsely settled country where he could easily put a bullet through my head without attracting attention. I wondered why he hadn't. Keeping me alive suggested he had some use for me.

"So what is the schedule?" I asked.

"Are you completely stupid, Mr. Doran?"

"Well, that does seem to be the consensus." I was in no position to argue with it.

"The schedule is now, Mr. Doran. It has begun."

"What, exactly?"

"She did not tell you? The Iranian woman?"

"Our conversation was interrupted," I reminded him.

"Does she know?"

"She said she did."

"Did you believe her?"

"What would be the point of lying to a nobody like me?"

"What indeed?" Gregoriev asked rhetorically and lapsed into brooding.

"So are you going to tell me about it?" I asked.

His smile was grim. "I shall do far better than that, Mr. Doran. I shall give you a role to play. You will become part of history. Not a history anyone would dare to write down, but history all the same."

I didn't like his emphasis on the word 'history'. I didn't ask any more questions. I couldn't think of any good ones and Gregoriev probably wouldn't have answered them anyway.

We had reached the Pass and he drove with the concentration of a man with things on his mind. I got one glimpse of the monastery through the trees, lofty and remote on its escarpment, and wondered if that was the spot where Lew Manders had lost his legs. A few kilometers beyond we left the pavement and started upslope. We made the camp in only two tire changes. This time I did the work while Gregoriev watched me and talked on a hand-held radio. The conversations were Russian and curt and I was able to glean nothing from them.

The camp was a bustling little place now, spread up the hillside for several hundred yards. The tents were gone. There was a perimeter of dug-in fighting positions and within that a few vehicles and a lot of equipment under camouflage nets. A guard passed us without challenge. Men working within the perimeter made way for us. Military bearing, slung Kalashnikovs and nonstop organized movement gave them the look of a military unit in spite of dreary peasant clothing. Gregoriev stopped the Land Cruiser. He got out and came around and opened the passenger door. I got out, glancing around to get my bearings.

A little distance away from the camouflaged supplies and the military hooligans, I saw a familiar figure. He sat on a low section of centuries' old ruin looking sullen and frustrated. I had found Alex Falkenberg.

Chapter 19

Finding Falkenberg here had an ominous air of closure. He was the one who sent me to Georgia to meet Eddington, who took me to the monastery where I bought a digital copy of the Alexandria Scrolls, and who then brought me to this camp. On that trip I barely escaped with my life. Gregoriev summed up my current survival prospects in one word.

"Plyenitsa," he barked at two nearby huskies. Russian for 'prisoner'.

Gregoriev's troopers were as agile as linebackers. They had me one by each arm before I could move. My feet didn't touch the ground more than twice on the trip across the hill to where Falkenberg sat. One of the huskies kicked my legs out from under me and both let go, depositing me like so much trash. They went off to see to less trivial chores. I sat on the cold ground nursing a new appreciation of how helpless and useless I was.

Falkenberg eyed me narrowly from his perch on the low remains of an ancient stone wall. "Just where the goddamn hell have you been?"

I got to my feet to muster some dignity. "Owen, old chum," I said in the faint hope of reminding him we were on the same side. "Good to see you're still in one piece. Bit of a pickle we're in here but--"

"Shut up."

The sources of his foul mood were obvious. The first was a chain around his leg fastening him to an iron post driven into the ground. When Falkenberg couldn't pace, he went nuts. The second was the fact that his high-end outdoor wardrobe had been slept in. For a man who hadn't bought even his underwear off the rack this century, that was a fate worse than death.

"Who knows you're here?" he asked with his uncanny sense of getting straight to the heart of any issue.

He winced when I told him Catherine Morse was the only person I'd reported my plans to. I didn't mention the fact that those plans had gone seriously awry.

"How did they catch you?" I asked.

"E-mail," he said. "Eddington needed me at the site. His driver would pick me up. Neglected to mention the Russian Army was here."

Being suckered was a new and disturbing experience for Falkenberg. For me, it was business as usual. I was more interested in a familiar figure coming across the slope toward us. For a man of his girth, Eddington made his way with remarkable dexterity. He had acquired some neatly groomed facial hair, a dress topcoat and a fedora since I had seen him last.

"Speak of the devil," I said.

"That's not Eddington."

I didn't quite say, "Huh?"

"The build is the same," Falkenberg said. "And he talks the same Brit crap. That's the only resemblance."

I was wrong about Eddington being a contradiction. I had never met Eddington. And I never would.

"Sebastian Eglik, I presume," I said when the newcomer arrived.

The man who had introduced himself as Professor Roald Eddington when I met him in Tblisi gave me a hard stare that went better with a one-time Turkish paratroop officer.

"You have heard that name where?" he inquired in his Oxford wheeze.

"Interpol," I said.

I reminded Falkenberg of Jerry's interrogation notes: a corpse found in Istanbul without head or hands identified as black market antiquities dealer Sebastian Eglik by comparing DNA with that of a tooth provided by Eglik's family. Prime suspect in the killing, Professor Roald Eddington.

"What did you do?" I asked Eglik. "Pull one of Eddington's teeth after you did him in? Have your relatives fob it off as one of yours? Fake your own death and assume his identity?"

A smuggler doing away with a professor made a lot more sense than Interpol's version. Eglik's scowl was indignant enough to tell me I had it wrong. He took out his Meerschaum and began to pack the bowl with tobacco, slowly and deliberately.

"I would not hesitate to kill in defense of my life," he informed me. "I might persuade myself to kill in a just cause. But I do not murder people. Particularly not my old school mates."

Accusing Eglik of murder wasn't too bright. He was liable to suggest to his Russian cohorts that I had already outlived my usefulness, whatever that might be. I gave him a contrite smile.

He put a match to his pipe.

"Roald telephoned with a tale of Georgian monks rescuing a hundred scrolls from the sack of the Library at Alexandria sixteen centuries ago. Some Russian chap had approached him with a scheme that might allow him to extract the Scrolls from the monastery where they were kept. Bit of a snag, though. Plan required dealing with the Russian Army. Not to Roald's taste. Not at all. But none of the soldiers had seen him. We looked a bit alike, and since I had military experience and he hadn't, he suggested an impersonation. If I pulled it off, I could broker the Scrolls. He came to Istanbul to finalize the arrangements. I found him dead and decapitated and I assumed his identity to carry forward the last enterprise of a dear friend."

It seemed important to Eglik that he be seen as honorable. An odd sentiment for a career criminal but I had no chance to puzzle over it. Two helicopters appeared in the distance, just above the treetops, flying the contours of the mountain side, growing louder as they neared our position. Upslope Gregoriev was gesturing and yelling into a radio. The helicopters slowed to a hover above him and settled to earth. Rotor downwash raised a massive dust cloud that spread to envelop the camp. I squinted and tried to keep from breathing any of it.

The rotors came to idle and the cloud subsided. The machines dominated the slope above, their multi-faceted windshields like the eyes of great filthy wind-borne insects. Neither carried any markings. Armed men in peasant garb disembarked, maybe twenty in all, lugging heavy packs. Several men on stretchers were put aboard. Following them were blanket wrapped bodies. The helicopters took off and Gregoriev went back to yelling into the radio as the dust rose around him.

"Poor chap," Eglik said when the machines were gone. "Terrified we'll be found out by the Georgian military. If either helicopter gets high enough to be picked up on radar, Major Gregoriev may spend the rest of his career as a Major."

Falkenberg stood to get in Eglik's face. "What the hell is going on here?"

Falkenberg was the taller man and his nostrils flared with angry breathing. Eglik was the more massive and had the composure that came with military service and discipline.

"Bit complicated, I'm afraid," Eglik said. "How's your knowledge of local politics?"

Falkenberg's only response was an impatient stare. I was in no mood for macho nonsense.

"He doesn't know shit," I said. "Neither of us do."

"You are aware," Eglik said, "that the Russians have had considerable trouble with Chechen terrorists. School children massacred. Airliners blown out of the sky."

"Get to the point," Falkenberg said.

"Chechen rebel headquarters is not many kilometers from here. In a place called Pankisi Gorge. The Gorge is in the Georgian Republic, just over the border with Chechnya and just out of reach of the regular Russian army. The situation calls for a spot of creativity on the part of the Russians. Forming new alliances. That sort of thing."

"Is there more to that?" Falkenberg demanded. "Or am I supposed to guess?"

"The Georgian Orthodox church," Eglik went on in an unruffled wheeze, "along with many denominations, Christian and non-Christian, has come under increasing pressure from the American Evangelical movement."

Falkenberg nodded. "Ten forty mafia."

That went over my head. I said, "What?" and Falkenberg gave me an irritated look.

"American evangelical churches have identified a band between ten degrees south latitude and forty degrees north latitude full of people ripe for conversion to their brand of Christianity."

Mary Ann and the Mighty Men came immediately to mind but I didn't say anything. I was more interested in what Eglik had to reveal than what I already knew.

"Existing churches," he said, "either find a way to match the invaders' spending or they watch their congregations dwindle."

"So the Georgian Orthodox Church sells off the Scrolls to stave off the competition," I said. "What do they need with a gang of Russians?"

Eglik shook his head. "Can't just sell off the Scrolls, dear boy. Selling the treasures, bad business, that. No end of repercussions. But if they happened to be lost in some terrorist skirmish, well--"

The Scrolls would vanish into the black market and a vandal military would be blamed. Shades of Julius Caesar and the siege of Alexandria.

"Why," Falkenberg asked, "would terrorists attack a two-bit monastery in the middle of nowhere?"

"Because the monastery physically dominates a key pass from Chechnya. Because Russian forces are in close proximity. Because the rebels have been fed months' worth of disinformation that the place has been turned into a Russian forward base for operations against Pankisi Gorge. All aimed at luring the Chechens into a fatal pre-emptive assault on the monastery and providing cover for the removal of the Scrolls."

Release of the Scrolls must have been in preparation for considerable time. Digitizing fragile old parchment had certainly been a long, painstaking process, but also an essential one in order to separate the actual artifacts from the translation that would establish their value on the black market. Falkenberg and I were just cogs in the machinery. Which raised the question of why Eglik had gone out of his way to talk to two prisoners.

"What do you want from us?" I asked.

"Gregoriev sent me to persuade you. And be assured, my dear Mr. Doran, that it is in your best interest to be persuaded."

"Of what?"

"You know Iranian Woman's time-table."

"She doesn't know her own time-table."

"I am quite serious, Mr. Doran."

"So am I. She wanted to know Gregoriev's schedule so she could plan her next move. Now he wants to know her schedule so he can plan his next move."

"Not good," Eglik said. "If Gregoriev can't deliver the Scrolls to his sponsors in Moscow, he and they will answer to the Russian Mafia."

Falkenberg snorted. "So if the Russian Mob doesn't get the Scrolls, some Iranian witch does. Where does that leave you?"

"Where I have always been. Following my instincts and living by my wits."

"How do we make a deal?" Falkenberg asked.

"Deal?" Eglik blinked.

"To get out of here. I'm not spending another night freezing my ass off on this fucking hill."

"No deal required, my dear fellow. We are all leaving for the monastery within the hour. Word is the Chechen assault force has already broken camp."

It didn't look like things could get any worse. I should have known better. Work in the camp stopped. Men up the hill from us began unslinging weapons. Others pointed into the sky. I looked in that direction.

I recognized the two planes. They were Czech made L-29s. They had been built during the cold war as jet trainers. Now obsolete, they were either sold to entrepreneurs in the U.S. as aviation toys or as weapons to third world air forces.

These two weren't toys. They were professionally flown ground attack fighters. They executed a neat formation turn and headed straight for us, wing tip to wing tip, not much above tree-top level. The Georgian military had arrived. And they were pissed.

A few idiots on the slope above tried shooting at the planes. Jets had an attack speed close to 400 miles an hour. A machine gun wasn't going to hit anything but air. I tackled Falkenberg, knocked him on his back and then jumped behind the low stone fortification, hoping it was still solid after three thousand years.

From the volume of incoming fire the L-29s had multi-barrel cannons in their gun packs. Bullets sizzled and cracked going above the wall that protected me, pocking the ground and cutting vegetation. The firing stopped. I risked a glance over the wall.

Both onrushing aircraft released bombs. Drag fins snapped out to retard the speed of the munitions and give the jets a chance to get out of the blast area. The planes went overhead, maybe fifty feet up. I felt the searing exhaust heat and the bone rattling thunder of the engines and I wondered if any of us would get off that hill alive.

Chapter 20

Bombs struck in rapid succession. The ground shuddered and the sky darkened. Debris began to crash down. Clumps of earth shattered, disgorging rocks in every direction. Whole trees and heavy limbs cracked and splintered on impact. I hunkered against the wall and waited to be hit by something big enough to kill me.

The cascade tapered away to a curtain of drifting smoke and dust. The sound of voices gave me the courage to look over the wall. Up the hill Gregoriev's troops were moving in response to shouted orders, tugging at toppled trees and clearing fallen camouflage netting. Falkenberg lurched to his feet, shaking off foliage like some creature rising from a primordial swamp. Eglik was already up, surveying the situation. It seemed to violate the laws of probability that volume gunfire had missed someone his size. The fact that we were away from the center of the camp probably had saved all three of us, although Eglik's fedora did seem worse for the experience when he clamped it on his head. He found a small brush in his pocket and began cleaning his Meerschaum. I decided it was safe to stand.

Two soldiers came down the hill and unlocked Falkenberg's chain. They herded the three of us upslope. We passed a medic trying to close off the gush of blood from a ruptured leg artery. A corpse lay tumbled against a tree, missing one arm and its head. I was glad I had passed on breakfast.

The camp's main stockpile of supplies and equipment had been thrown into random heaps. A strapping Russian ordered us to help a group of soldiers sort through the mess. Eglik tried to excuse himself from the work party. That earned him a sharp poke with the muzzle of a rifle. I pitched in without an argument.

The job involved retrieving pack boards. Each had a two foot long metal cylinder strapped to it. The cylinders were robust without being ponderous. The huskies in the work party could have slung them around easily but they handled them as gingerly as china.

"What has these guys spooked?" I asked Eglik.

"They know from training that the gas is binary but they do not know how much damage the bombing may have done."

The cylinders had fragments of Cyrillic script on them but nothing I could make out as words. "Could you be a little more specific about this binary gas concept?"

"Transport of fully constituted nerve agents is an unacceptable risk," Eglik said as he hoisted a pack board. "The slightest accident could wipe out your entire force. So the gas is subdivided into two components, each harmless by itself. When the time comes to deploy them, a small explosive charge breaches the partition between the components and the resulting reaction releases the agent."

Unless the Georgian Air Force had done the job first. I jumped back from the pack board I had been tugging on.

A Russian trooper caught me by the scruff of the neck and pushed me back to work. Eglik emitted a wheezing laugh. It seemed to be painful for him. He washed down a pill with a swig from a pocket flask before he spoke.

"Had the bombing damaged the cylinders, nothing on this hill would be alive," he assured me.

"The Chechens," Falkenberg realized, "are walking into a death trap. As soon as they take over the monastery, gas bombs start going off all over the place. Just like that theater business in Moscow."

There never was any intention to re-open the dig site. The Russian military went to Silmenov to provide cover for their operation. He turned them down. Eddington didn't. He wanted the Scrolls and this was a way to get them out of the monastery. He lost his nerve and his life and Eglik stepped into his shoes. None of which explained what Falkenberg and I were doing there.

"Why drag the Foundation into this?" I asked.

"If the archaeological dig is sponsored by a well-connected American foundation, CIA involvement will be assumed. American forces are, after all, fighting Chechen contingents in Afghanistan."

"And Alex and I participating personally removes any possibility that we were innocent dupes?" I asked.

Eglik was in no mood to belabor the obvious. His humor worsened when a soldier ordered the three of us to shoulder pack boards. Eglik marched over to Gregoriev to complain. Bad move. Gregoriev was looking for someplace to vent his frustrations. My Russian wasn't good enough to keep up with his tirade but he sent Eglik away with his tail between his legs.

Things had changed in the past two weeks. The shooting during my first visit to the camp had likely been staged for a couple of reasons. First to kill me, which would cut the Foundation, and by extension the Scalded Woman, out of the running for the Scrolls while leaving an unmistakable American fingerprint on the whole business. Second to give the impression that Chechen forces were prowling outside Pankisi Gorge, which would make the attack on the monastery seem part of a pattern. Eglik and the Russians had been in cahoots then. Now it looked like it was every scheming crook for himself.

"Wild guess," I said when Eglik rejoined us. "Gregoriev's plan works better if you, Falkenberg and I aren't around afterward to discuss what we've seen?"

Eglik adjusted a shoulder bag he had taken time to retrieve from his luggage and hoisted a pack board onto his back.

"I know of no military plan in this or any other century that has survived the firing of the first bullet," was all he had to say.

Gregoriev had plenty to say. In ten minutes he had the seriously wounded under camouflage with a medic to do what little he could for them. The rest of us, maybe eighty men in all, were organized into a ramshackle line of march.

"Why is he pushing us?" I asked Eglik as we started down the trail toward the pass.

"The two jets that strafed us were second line scout aircraft dispatched from the nearest forward base to investigate the radar sighting of the helicopters. If the Georgian Air Force decides to follow up, they will sortie front line aircraft, purpose built for ground attack, with sufficient warloads to obliterate us. Particularly if they catch us in the open."

There wasn't much doubt the Georgian Air Force would find us if they came looking. A column of heavily laden men making their slow way down a track wide enough to pass vehicles would be obvious from the air. Separating myself wasn't an option. Not only was Gregoriev moving along the line with relentless energy, exhorting his men to make speed, he also had riflemen out as security on either flank. I wondered if Eglik had a plan to get himself out of this predicament.

"You're on the wrong side of this squabble, aren't you?" I asked

"What do you mean?"

"According to Interpol, you're Muslim."

"My father schooled me in the ways of Islam. Over the objections of my very Christian mother. When I grew to manhood, Islam became my faith of choice."

"And yet here you are with the Crusaders. Marching to wipe out the Chechen Muslims."

"You are very badly read in history, dear boy."

I didn't bother to argue. First because I was preoccupied keeping my balance on the rocky slope. Second because I had heard the phrase on my first trip to Georgia. It was a prelude to one of Eglik's lectures.

"It was the Ottoman Empire," he began solemnly, "that spread Islam. It was their civilization and military organization that brought it to the gates of Europe and beyond. But corruption came, and the greatest corruption of all was oil. It was found not in the civilized land of Turkey, but under the feet of Bedouins. Nomads who subsisted on the meat and milk of whatever pathetic animals they could contrive to keep alive. It was on them that the world heaped its wealth until the One True Faith fell under the stewardship of wandering goatherds. Buffoons parading about in flowing robes and lavishing money on any thug who pretends to the creed of Allah."

It sounded like Islam was as fragmented as Christianity. Everyone belonged to their own little clique and nobody liked anyone else.

"Justice will come," Eglik assured me. "The oil will run out. But until the goatherds slide back into the poverty and ignorance from which they arose, all believers are obligated to oppose their perversion of The Faith."

"Even if it's only as a pack mule for the Russian Army?" I asked.

"Are you one of these chaps who go to military cinema and imagines himself in charge of great armies in pivotal battles?"

It was less embarrassing to let silence do my fessing up.

"In reality," he said, "not one of the feeble spectators sitting in air conditioned comfort would qualify as even a foot soldier in history's great battles. Had they lived then, they would have been just what you and I are today. Conscript labor. Drudges in a supply train, enduring hours of back-breaking labor in the faint hope they would reach the community kitchen while something remotely edible remained."

Eglik's lecture was as unproductive as it was depressing. Falkenberg was behind me in the column. There were a couple of Gregoriev's troopers between us but when it came to clumsy I was a natural. A little creative stumbling put me beside him. I kept my voice low.

"Any ideas how we get out of this?"

"Authority figures are the biggest suckers in the world," he said. "They've all got their eye on the next rung up the ladder. I know people who know people who can make Major Gregoriev a General."

Assuming we weren't all shot dead in the next ten minutes. "Have you talked to him?"

"Keep shut until we get to the monastery," Falkenberg ordered. "I want Gregoriev with the Scrolls in hand before I put the deal to him."

It was vintage Falkenberg. We were walking out of one death trap into another and he wanted to wheel and deal. Gregoriev called a halt at the bottom of the hill. I needed the rest but I didn't need the thoughts that came with it. I saw no escape from the situation, no way to deal with it, only the very real possibility that I was trudging to the end of an undistinguished life.

The hike to the monastery was upslope. My pack board seemed to gain twenty pounds. The trail was steeper, the stones were looser and the Russians behind me were getting cranky. Eventually I lost interest in their pushing and cursing. I could no longer feel my feet and went on faith that they were still at the ends of my ankles. The pack harnesses bit into my shoulders and held my parka tightly in place, trapping the heat of exertion and soaking me in sweat. Even as we drew near I could see the monastery only dimly through the steam on my glasses.

Eglik appeared beside me. "Warn your friend Falkenberg not to talk to the Monks about the Scrolls."

I managed a strangled laugh. Warning Falkenberg was like waving meat at a ravenous hound.

"I am serious, dear boy. Instructions to surrender the monastery and the Scrolls come from the Church Fathers. The monks are ill-disposed to cede the home and the treasure they have given their lives over to protecting. Obedience will test their faith sorely. They await us with hostile hearts, and they need little temptation to stray."

There was no doubt we were expected. Friar Bones was waiting at the oak doors when we arrived, all skeletal seven feet of him, scourging every sinner who passed into this house of God with his smoldering eyes.

"You are a fool to return," he told me.

I wouldn't have argued with him even if I weren't spent. We went into the courtyard and dropped our packs. I slumped down with my back against mine. If I was going to die, this was probably as good a place as any.

Chapter 21

ll-focused bustle filled the courtyard. The accompanying voices were vague and uneven in volume, like the sound track of a foreign movie. A shadow fell over me. Something hard jabbed my chest. I mustered the effort to take off my glasses.

The shadow was one of the Russians. He swore at me and prodded me with the muzzle of his rifle. It hurt but I had no energy to respond. It didn't matter that he prodded me again. It didn't matter whether he shot me. I just sat there, drained.

He gave up, jerked the pack board out from behind me and lugged it off. A parched throat suggested my shortcomings in the will-to-live department might have something to do with dehydration. I wiped the fog off my glasses, put them back on and forced myself to my feet to find something to drink.

Shambling along the colonnade brought me to a heavy canvas sack suspended from a tripod. Metal drinking cups hung from little spouts around the bottom. Thirst left me trembling to the point that I spilled as much water as I got into the cup. The liquid turned my tongue sour and left icicles in my esophagus. The shock dissipated my stupor. I drank some more and began to develop an interest in my surroundings.

The nerve gas cylinders were lined up in neat ranks out in the courtyard, like rows of little soldiers on a parade ground. One Spetnatz trooper worked his way along the ranks, using a wrench to attach what was probably a fuse to each. Work parties carried cylinders into the surrounding buildings as he finished.

Across the courtyard Eglik was talking to the head monk. They were too far away for me to hear but body language spoke volumes. The monk was still and serene. Eglik was more animated than I had ever seen him. He was waving his Meerschaum at the old gentleman when a rattle of automatic gunfire froze him. I ducked behind a column.

Two more staccato bursts established that the gunfire was outside the walls. NCOs barked orders. Troopers snatched up weapons and gear and scrambled to defend the entrance. Others dashed into buildings only to reappear at defensive positions along the outer wall above the rooftops. I heard a commotion at the oak doors.

A five-man patrol erupted from the passageway into the courtyard. Two men supported one who had been wounded. The oak doors closed, filling the passage with darkness. Defenders scrambled out and the portcullis came down behind them. Gregoriev held a brief conference with the patrol leader and then gave orders for everyone to gather in the courtyard. I joined the assembly.

Falkenberg appeared out of nowhere and spoke in my ear. "Not looking good," he said in an uncharacteristically somber tone. "I'm afraid the military types have screwed up even worse than usual."

Gregoriev addressed his troops and the Monks in Russian. I was able to get the gist. Estimates of the strength of Chechen forces in Pankisi gorge had been more than a little low. Revised numbers indicated we would be facing about ten times our strength. We had also been a little late in moving. The monastery was surrounded. The rest of the speech was pep talk. A rough translation was death before dishonor. The head monk stepped up and offered absolution to those who were about to give their lives in defense of the Faith. Falkenberg was Jewish and I was a recovering Presbyterian so neither of us took him up on it.

Most of the Spetnatz troopers did. The few who didn't were apparently Muslims. Eglik addressed them and they all knelt and bowed to Mecca. His military experience had shaped him to a greater extent than I realized. He meant to take a hand in the game. I looked at Falkenberg.

Sweat had left streaks down the dirty stubble on his sagging jowls. His weight had turned from bulk to burden. His eyes had lost none of their resolve but he was no better suited to physical stress that I was.

"Are you in this fight?" I asked.

"Did you ever see the old Jean-Claude Van Damm groaner *Legionnaire?*" he asked.

He was right. We had no choice. We would hold out to the last man standing and hope for a miracle. In the end it wouldn't matter. The Chechens would take the fort, massacre the defenders and die sucking nerve gas for their trouble. Russian troops had already resumed the task of placing the cylinders.

Friar Bones opened the monastery arsenal and we lined up with the monks to draw weapons. Eglik requested and received the sole FN assault rifle. He was still carrying the shoulder bag he had brought from the camp.

"Planning a trip?" I asked.

"The will of Allah shall come to pass," he informed me. "Even here in the bastion of the infidel. Those of us privileged to follow him can only prepare ourselves and wait."

He bid Falkenberg and me good luck and strode off to join the Spetnatz contingent, mustering more military carriage than a man of his girth had any right to show. Something was driving him but I had no clue what it was.

The monks took all the AK-47s, leaving a couple of old semi-automatic SKS carbines. Friar Bones gave Falkenberg and me a quick operating demonstration. He handed the loaded weapon to Falkenberg and sent him off with a monk to show him his position. I got a rattier example and a bandolier of ammunition.

"Do you have a water bottle?" I asked. "A canteen? Anything like that?" I didn't want another bout of dehydration.

He found a small metal flask with a screw-on cap. It had lived a hard life in unclean places but my long term health probably wasn't an issue anyway. And something else was nagging at me.

"I guess the Scrolls have already been moved to someplace safe," I said.

"For thirteen hundred years they have rested here," Friar Bones said. "Waiting until God had need of them." He took a Luger from a drawer and began charging the magazine.

"The idea of killing someone," I asked, "it doesn't bother you?"

"Because the storms of chance have blown my life into the service of God I should be troubled by his commandments?"

I shrugged in general agreement. His laugh was mocking and humorless.

"God knows the sins of my days and the evil I have never been able to banish from my heart. If he has sent me to this place then this is where he needs such things. It is my lot and that of my brothers to provide according to His will."

"Life is a speed bump on the road to heaven?" I asked.

"We expect no reward from God. We serve Him. He does not serve us. And if the price of that service is Hell, then let it be so."

"So God keeps you around to confront his enemies? Is that the deal?"

His eyes scolded me with contempt. "Only a fool confronts his enemy. Sneak on him. Shoot him behind. Never brag what you do."

He tucked the Luger and a spare magazine into the folds of his robe and exchanged a few words in Georgian with two monks who were maneuvering a crate of 37 millimeter anti-aircraft ammunition out the door. We followed them.

The courtyard was empty. The sky had dulled and drizzle began to fall. Friar Bones gave me a minute to fill the flask from the canvas bag and then led me into a dim building, up a narrow flight of stairs and along a succession of twisting passages. Nerve gas canisters lurked in the half-light, wired and ready to go off. I would never find my way back out without tripping one of the booby traps.

We came out onto the roof. A walkway joined defensive positions along the outer wall of the monastery; niches built centuries ago for archers. Most were occupied by Spetnatz troops. Friar Bones deposited me at an empty one and went on toward the ruined tower, leaving me alone and discouraged. I risked a look out the niche.

The monastery walls were thirty feet tall and the ground on the other side of the ravine at the bottom fell away into a forest. From my perch movement was visible down in the mist that was settling among the trees. I didn't know if Gregoriev was right about the exact odds but the fog-shrouded phalanx making its way up the slope gave his estimate serious credibility. I doubted any Chechen goons would care that I didn't give a rat's ass about East European politics.

The niche to my right was held by a strapping Russian with a wide grin. He was making adjustments to a complex weapon. I had seen pictures of it in books. A Dragunov sniper rifle. He gave me a thumbs-up and said something incomprehensible in a heavy Slavic accent. All I had to offer was a mousey smile.

The Russian leaned into his niche and put the Dragunov into action. The deliberate pop-pop of rifle fire banished my last vestige of denial. Owen Doran's moment of truth had arrived. I ducked down to get ready.

From what Friar Bones had shown us, loading the SKS was accomplished by retracting the bolt, inserting a ten round stripper clip and pushing the contents down into the magazine. He had pulled it off in one smooth stroke.

I didn't.

My hand was trembling. It took several tries to get the stripper clip mounted. When I pushed down, three rounds loaded and then the whole mess came apart. I had to put the other seven in one at a time.

By the time I finished my fellow defenders were exchanging volume small arms fire with the advancing Chechens. The monastery's anti-aircraft gun opened slow automatic fire from the tower, the muzzle depressed to send explosive shells down the slope. I gathered what courage I could and rose up in my niche.

The Chechens were closer now, visible as individual figures struggling against the slope and the undergrowth. One looked like he was giving orders. My authority issues kicked in and I took an instant dislike to him. He became a proxy for every boss I had ever had. Everyone who ever bullied me. Everyone who ever told me what to do. I had found my target.

The sights on the SKS were the same blade-and-notch variety as on the old .22 Grandpa Doran had taught me to shoot. He had been very disappointed in me. I could hit matchbook covers at fifty yards but I refused to hunt rabbits. I would never be a real man. I lined up the SKS to take my revenge on the world of authority and show the old fart what I was made of.

An automatic rifle burst rattled off the stone inches from my head and scared the shit out of me. My shot went wild and I ducked behind the wall.

Chapter 22

I sat shivering with my back pressed against the stone wall. I was going to die among strangers. Ten thousand miles from home. Murdered in a meaningless skirmish. No one would know it had happened. I would just turn up missing and that would be that. If anyone bothered to look, the trail would peter out in Tblisi. I fumbled off my glasses and wiped away the accumulated drizzle.

The situation didn't look any better through clean lenses. Flight was pointless. Every niche along the parapet was manned by a Spetnatz trooper who wouldn't take kindly to desertion. Not that there was any place to desert to. Every door led to a booby trapped canister of nerve gas. Below my niche a tile roof sloped steeply down to a gutter. I saw only a bone-breaking drop from there into the courtyard.

Across the compound Eglik was braced in his own niche. The recoil of the FN jolted his bulk with each round he fired. He was totally absorbed; a venal degenerate by normal standards, doing his part in a hopeless cause with no visible thought to his own safety. Every niche had its own story, a monk or a Spetnatz trooper, each overcoming personal desires and demons to contribute what he could to a common goal. Every niche but mine. Alone and left out was the story of my life, but I usually didn't inflict it on myself. It wasn't the way I wanted things to end. I got a grip on my rifle, wormed up the wall to a crouch and moved my head just enough to peek out the niche.

The hill below was crawling with men, firing as they advanced, slipping from bush to rock to tree, using every fold in the rugged ground as cover. The geometry of my niche might allow me to risk a shot across the slope without exposing much more than the SKS. It wasn't until I tried to align the sights that I realized I was still shivering. Pressing myself hard against the stone wall, I managed to stabilize enough to square up the front sight blade in the notch.

The rifle bucked against my shoulder. A man beyond the man I was aiming at went down and came back up hobbling. As victories went it wasn't much but it was a ray of hope. Maybe I wasn't useless. I tried another shot.

There was no visible result. I needed to settle down. Steady the rifle. Make every shot count. I felt the next round buck against my shoulder and the next and the next. The acrid smoke of firing infiltrated my nostrils. Heat from the chamber shimmered in my line of sight and repeated blasts dimmed my hearing. The bolt locked open on an empty magazine and I ducked down to reload.

Concussion shook the monastery. Dust and smoke rose out of the courtyard down and away from my position. The Chechens had managed to lob some kind of explosive shell inside the walls. The dust settled and the smoke dissipated and I didn't see any damage. In fact, the whole attack didn't seem to be making much headway. Even if life was cheap and martyrdom treasured, throwing cannon fodder at high stone walls protected by a bottomless ravine wasn't much of a strategy. The Chechens wouldn't have come without a solid plan to breach the monastery's defenses. I finished loading the rifle and wormed up into the niche to take a better look.

The answer was on the access road. A crew was manhandling an unwieldy recoilless cannon into shooting position. That was why the Chechens had attacked in daylight. The cannon was a direct fire weapon. It would be difficult to aim from stand-off range at night. After seeing what Spetnatz's version had done to the iron gate of The Scalded Woman's villa in Tblisi, I didn't give the monastery's oak doors much chance. I lined up the SKS to see if I could pick off the crew.

It was a long shot and steeply downhill from my perch on the monastery wall. I didn't even get their attention. I tried two more shots with the same result. I was cursing my own inadequacy when it dawned on me that the man in the next niche was a Russian Army sniper with state-of-the-art equipment. All I needed to do was get his attention and get the Dragunov pointed in the right direction. I pulled back from my niche.

That was as far as my brilliant plan got. Spetnatz's sniper would be no danger to the men wrestling the cannon. The bullet had taken him in the forehead, not quite squarely. He appeared to have gone slack and oozed down the wall until he was sitting on his own legs. One side of his face was pressed against the stone. His mouth hung open and his eyes were vacant. He looked like a moron who had forgotten what he wanted to say. I clenched my throat against the rebellion in my stomach and crawled toward him to recover the Dragunov.

Heavy boots blocked my path. A thick paw came down and snatched up the sniper rifle. Gregoriev stood over me. I scrambled to my feet.

"Cannon!" I yelled into his face, pointing out the niche, and the Russian equivalent, "Pushka!" when that got me nothing but a glare.

He snarled something like, "Stryela," which I thought was Russian for shoot.

"Look down on the access road. The Chechens are training a cannon on the gate. Cannon. Pushka. Varota."

He grabbed my parka with his free hand and shoved me into my niche. He was a strong son-of-a-bitch and the impact knocked the air out of my lungs. Most of what he growled at me was probably profanity. The little I caught translated roughly to fight or die.

He was gone before I recovered enough wind to mount an argument. Sucking in chill air got my brain functioning again. Gregoriev had known about the cannon. He had come to make sure his sniper didn't pick off the crew. If the Chechens didn't breach our defenses, the nerve gas would never have a chance to do its work. I wasn't part of that plan so I lined up the SKS to see what I could do to frustrate it.

At least the cannon and the crew were stationary now as they made final preparations for their shot. I emptied the magazine, firing each shot more carefully than the last. It was a waste of effort. I ducked back down to reload.

Two grim-faced monks passed my position, schlepping a heavy crate of ammunition up to the anti-aircraft gun.

"The cannon!" I yelled at them. "On the road. Tell the gun crew to shoot at the cannon!"

No response.

Another Chechen shell exploded down in the courtyard, closer this time, and I ducked and covered. When I looked up again, the monks were gone. Across the courtyard I saw empty niches where there had been defenders. I was no tactician, but I had seen enough war movies to guess what was going on. Gregoriev wasn't above doing a little evil in the name of Mother Russia but he wasn't planning to commit suicide in the process. He was thinning the defenses, leaving a few men to hold the walls while he gathered an assault force to break out. Naturally any worthless Americans could be sacrificed for the effort.

Suddenly I was back in junior high school. They were picking baseball teams in Physical Ed.

"How come we get Owen?"

"Everybody has to play."

"He can't do nothing."

"He's useless."

"Put him in the outfield. Maybe he'll luck out and catch something."

It wasn't a baseball that arced over my head. It was a grenade. I scrunched myself into the smallest ball I could manage.

The grenade bounced on the steep roof behind me, dropped into the courtyard and exploded harmlessly. I rose into the niche again. Bullets rattled off the stone walls like metal balls in a pachinko game. The assault was rising to a crescendo to cover the cannon shot. The advancing Chechens were close enough to see clearly now, real people with faces twisted by fear and exertion, their eyes mad with the fury of combat. I steadied the rifle in the niche, firing slowly and deliberately and then ducking down to reload.

A Russian, probably some sort of non-commissioned officer, was moving toward me along the wall, stopping at each remaining position to exhort the man there to greater effort. I was reading his lips more than hearing him. My ears were ringing and the noise of battle seemed far away. I stood to block him as he drew close and leveled my rifle to make sure he stopped.

"Where are the others?" I demanded in my best Russian.

He started in on a tirade. He never had a chance to finish. One of the Chechens had finally zeroed in my niche. The Russian caught a three round burst. One blew through his neck and spread high-velocity spatter. Another broke his jaw and sent teeth and bits of cheek flying. The third went through his head and blew the other side of his skull out. He collapsed, dead before he landed. I froze against the wall.

No noise came from the tower. The anti-aircraft gun had been secured. Everyone was headed for the emergency exit. Except me. I had no clue where it was.

The back-blast of the recoilless cannon lit the gathering dusk outside. The shell hit the main doors and blew shards of oak and a massive cloud of dust through the entry passage and the iron portcullis and into the courtyard. The end game had begun. I could either die where I stood or make the most of the long odds against getting away. I jumped down to the steeply pitched roof below.

The surface was slick with drizzle. I slid down rather than running, flailing all the way, and spilled over the gutter. I knew I was going to land hard.

Chapter 23

The impact spilled me sideways. The fact that I was able to regain my feet told me I hadn't fractured any important bones. Staying upright was my next challenge. My surroundings lost focus. The ground tipped and rolled like a carnival ride. I grabbed one of the ornate columns for support and hung on while I coughed dust and phlegm out of my throat.

Smoke burned my eyes and obscured the courtyard. There seemed to be some activity at the far end. I pushed off from my column and stumbled that way as fast as my shaky balance would allow, driven by the fear that I would be left to die.

The activity turned out to be a casualty collection point tucked into the shelter of the colonnade. Blood made a slippery coat on the mosaic. Stained remnants of clothing were strewn everywhere. Bandaged men lay on stretchers or sat against the walls. The stench was overwhelming. I backed away.

Battle had turned the courtyard into a minefield of shell holes and fallen stones. In the midst of it all stood Sebastian Eglik; a solitary figure in the dregs of chaos, mounting his heavy FN on a pile of rubble so it was trained on the portcullis. I made my way over to him.

"What's the plan?" I yelled in his ear.

He peered for a minute before he recognized me. "If anyone was dead by now," he said in a tortured wheeze, "I thought it would be you. One of these survivor chaps, are you? Get out of any fix by blind luck?"

If I had any luck, I never would have gotten into this mess. "What's going on?" I asked. "What are they up to?"

"Breaking out, dear boy."

"Can you be a little more specific?"

"Gregoriev's got it in his head that he's going to break through the Chechen encirclement at their time of greatest weakness, when they have drawn down their security forces to mount the assault. He hasn't the men to do it, even if he did know the Chechen order of battle, but there's no talking to a Russian when he's got hold of an idea."

It was a lot to say and it left him puffing. He sat on the pile of rubble, dug out a bottle of pills and took one dry. I threw a nervous glance at the portcullis.

"That Chechen assault is already overdue."

Eglik let out a caustic laugh. "No real military training, eh? Just books and cinema full of handsome, pathetic heroes."

"Could you fill me in? High level summary?"

"Do you know what a Bangalore torpedo is?" he asked.

"Sections of pipe filled with explosives," I recalled dimly from one of the books full of handsome, pathetic heroes. "They can be screwed together and pushed ahead of advancing troops to blow holes in barbed wire obstacles and explode buried mines."

"The Chechens have to expect booby traps in the entry passage. They'll fire off a Bangalore before they send in sappers to blow the portcullis and infantry to take the ground."

Straight from some stuffy British military mess. Neat and tidy, and very immediate.

"So what exactly are you planning to do?"

"Some of the wounded are mine. At least my brothers in devotion to Allah. Thought I'd buy them a little time. Just in case Gregoriev has a stroke of luck."

I would have laughed if he weren't dead serious. He was fifty plus out-of-breath years and three hundred lumbering pounds of Oxford educated crook and he was planning to go down fighting in a war of thugs.

"What about the Scrolls?" I asked.

"For that, Allah has sent me you."

He stood, unslung the bag from his shoulder and hung it around my neck before I could protest.

"What's in here?" I asked.

"The proof, dear boy. Fragments that the scientific chaps with their radio carbon procedures and spectroscopes and cyclotrons can use to establish that the disc full of knowledge the monks gave you is real."

"Why don't you take them out?"

"At some point, dear boy, we all return to our first love. Mine is history. Always has been. Never had a chance to make any myself. Not until now. Don't want to pass it up."

That was nonsense and we both knew it.

He took out his Meerschaum and a tobacco pouch. Right in the middle of a shell-scarred courtyard, with the pop of rifle fire from the surrounding walls. I watched him load the pipe and put that together with his wheezy voice and the pills he was taking.

"How bad is it?" I asked to test my theory.

"As situations go," he said, "this one couldn't get much worse."

"The cancer," I said. "How bad is your cancer?"

He let me wait while he fired the pipe. Maybe he just needed the time to get up the nerve to talk about it.

"Bearable, for now. In two years I will have nothing left that would qualify as a throat, if the doctors are to be believed. The pain medicines will grow ever less effective and I will grow ever more melancholy."

"So you've decided to cash in here?"

"Pass no judgment," he wheezed. "At least not until the day comes when you too will walk in my shoes."

It was a chilling prospect that left me feeling small and insignificant. Like Eglik, I was doomed to spend whatever time remained to me trying to make the best of a situation beyond my control.

"Do you know where the Scrolls are?" I asked.

He was shaking his head when the blast came. I guessed it was a Bangalore torpedo. I had never seen one go off but a cloud of debris blew through the portcullis and billowed toward us.

Eglik hunkered behind the pile of rubble and put the rifle to his shoulder. "Go now and you may find your Scrolls some day. Stay and you will only die."

I didn't need to be told twice.

The casualty collection point was evacuating fast. A monk was gesturing for someone to take the other end of a stretcher. The casualty wasn't anyone I recognized. He didn't matter. The monk knew the way and I didn't. The stretcher was my ticket out of the monastery. I slung my rifle and grabbed the handles.

A doorway let us into a poorly lit passage. Stone stairs took us down into the bowels of the building. The slow thunder of Eglik's FN penetrated the ringing in my ears, punctuated by the crumps of explosions. The Chechens were blowing the portcullis. A savage crescendo of automatic gunfire from the courtyard filled me with dread. Once the Chechens overran the place, nerve gas bombs would start going off all over. The gas would spread broadcast. It wouldn't care who it killed. The passage was narrow and I could go no faster than the stretcher ahead of me.

At the bottom of the stairs a door hung open into the gathering gloom outside. The head monk stood there, seeing the last of his flock out of the doomed complex. If the place needed a metaphor, he was it. A serene old gentleman holding a Bible in one hand and a Browning automatic in the other. We maneuvered the stretcher past him. I had no idea what lay ahead and I hoped his blessing had nothing to do with last rites.

Outside was a meager trail demarcated by granite that rose steeply one side and fell away into bottomless dusk on the other. Rough ground slickened by drizzle made the footing treacherous. Pronounced downslope turned gravity into an enemy. It took all my strength to stay upright and not lose control of my end of the stretcher.

I don't know when I became aware of the silence. Silence wasn't even the right word. My ears were still ringing but there was no more gunfire. No more explosions. No more sound of life from the monastery. I didn't know if the people inside were actually dead. No one had mentioned how the gas worked. Whether it was quick and painless or a drawn out agony of convulsions as the central nervous system shut down. I didn't have time to think about it.

The trail bottomed out and we started up. My arms ached and my feet throbbed. Sweat fogged my glasses. Not that it mattered. Nightfall was close enough that only shadows were visible. I didn't know how the monk on the other end of the stretcher found his way. I struggled to keep up.

The ground grew less steep. Blackness closed in and the smell of forest grew pungent. Vegetation snatched at my arms and tried to wrap itself around the sling of my rifle and the strap of Eglik's shoulder bag. I remembered his admonition that Gregoriev hadn't the men needed to break the Chechen encirclement.

The Chechens had to be close. Probably just out of rifle range from the monastery walls. My imagination filled the surrounding forest with shadowy hobgoblins waiting their chance to snatch me away. All I could do was keep my grip on the stretcher and wonder how long my legs and my lungs would hold out.

Light flickered through the trees, silhouetting the column of men ahead. As we drew closer I could make out hooded figures with shrouded lanterns. Trucks were lined up in parallel ruts that made a road through the forest. Stake-beds of various manufacture, six by my count, all laden with crates. The treasures of the monastery, I guessed, but I didn't dare ask. I kept my breathing as quiet as I could.

Our stretcher was passed up to men on the last vehicle. One of them looked our passenger over with a dim light. The trip probably hadn't helped him. It had taken the stuffing out of me. I would have collapsed, if I dared, but the chances of being left behind were too great to risk resting.

A murmur made its way among the monks. They started climbing onto the backs of the trucks. Friar Bones got into the cab of an old GMC. I spent the last of my energy pulling myself up on the back and collapsed among the crates piled there.

I had two monks for company. Both were armed.

"Russki?" one asked in a low whisper.

"American."

Another clicked a fresh magazine into his AK-47. "Do you speak English?" he asked in a voice that gave me a good idea what would happen if I didn't have the right answer.

"All the time," I assured him.

There didn't seem to be any more objections to my presence. I unslung my rifle so I could sink down into a protective depression in the crates.

One of the monks reached over and shoved the contents of a stripper clip into the empty magazine. He pivoted the bayonet folded against the barrel until it locked outward in combat position. He touched a finger to the tip and then to my throat. He touched the toe of the rifle butt, then the side of my head. Bayonet fighting in two easy lessons. I hadn't given much thought to the mechanics of assaulting the Chechen encirclement but it was becoming obvious it wouldn't be a pleasant experience.

Underscoring the point was a passenger I hadn't noticed at first. He was on a stretcher wedged down between two crates. Probably one of the Russians. He clutched an assault rifle across his chest. His breathing was an uncertain rasp. I heard him choke back a moan.

The lanterns went out. Night swallowed us whole. Time passed and the drizzle turned to rain. Sweat turned to ice inside my clothes and I had to work to keep my teeth from chattering. I began to cramp from the enforced stillness. No one said a word or moved a muscle. My mind began to drift. I wondered what had happened to Falkenberg. I wondered if I would ever sit in front of a computer again or add a column of numbers or tinker with my Honda or any of the thousand other little things I had always taken for granted. I wondered if I would see the sun shine again.

An explosion jolted me back to reality. It was close enough to hear but not close enough to see. Automatic gunfire erupted from the same direction. Truck engines started. I wanted to yell at them to wait. I wasn't ready. It was too late. The GMC lurched into motion and jolted me back against a crate.

Chapter 24

The gunfire tapered away with no hint of whether one side had won or both had gone to ground in the pitch black forest. The only sounds were the grumbling of exhaust pipes and the creak of over-burdened suspensions. A flash and a pop issued from back in the convoy. There was a softer pop overhead, followed by filtered light. The light grew brighter as a parachute flare descended slowly out of the low clouds. Trees loomed close on either side and branches overhung the dirt track, stark and grotesque beneath the artificial radiance, their shadows groping at the slow moving trucks. I cursed the stupidity of whoever had revealed our position.

As usual, I was wrong. The monks had anticipated a roadblock and launched the flare to spot it. A tree had been felled, choking the track with tangled limbs. The lead truck was fitted with something resembling a snowplow. It wedged its way through the branches, burying itself past the cab in foliage, and engaged the tree trunk with its angle iron. An immovable weight of nature against the irresistible force of soviet-era technology. I listened to wheels spin in vain.

Friar Bones eased the front bumper of the GMC against the snowplow's back bumper to add our horsepower and traction. The fallen tree began to move, pivoting reluctantly around its own stump. Then the flare fizzled out into darkness. Voices issued from the forest. Dread chilled me down to my marrow. I tightened my grip on the SKS.

Truck headlights came on and lit the track and the flanking trees as a mass of Chechens broke cover. The attackers swarmed the snowplow from both sides, yelling and shooting. Three monks and a couple of Spetnatz casualties were sheltered among the crates on the back. They put up a fight, firing full automatic into the Chechen onslaught and bayoneting anyone who tried to climb aboard. With its front bumper hard against the rear of the snowplow, the GMC was the next logical target. I felt the assault before I saw it.

The GMC shuddered on its springs as unseen men clambered up the sides. A face rose out of the night right in front of me, seamed and ill-shaven in the glare of headlights, an animal countenance, eyes on fire with violence. Terror overwhelmed the monk's bayonet fighting lesson and I drove the SKS forward.

The blade ripped into the man's cheek, grazing his nose and just beneath one eye. He screamed and seized the rifle barrel while he hung onto the side of the truck with his other hand. He tried to wrench the SKS out of my grasp with the bayonet still embedded. The weapon discharged. The flash seared his eye and the bullet lifted tangled hair going out through the back of his head. The bayonet came free. The Chechen went slack and fell away. His comrades boiled up over the sides of the GMC. I got off two point blank shots before I was knocked onto my back.

One of the Chechens came down at me with a knife, his face full of triumph at an easy victory. I drew my knees up, slammed the soles of my boots against his chest and shoved with a full jolt of adrenaline, launching him over the side of the truck. A struggle raged above me. Through a forest of legs I saw more trouble on the front fenders of the GMC.

There was a Chechen clinging to each. They were trying to get the hood up. If they succeeded, all chance of escape would vanish. The man on the passenger side was closer. The shot I triggered hit him hard enough to knock him off the fender. Before I could line up on the second, the boot of one of the men struggling above me came down on the rifle and pinned it to a crate. I was reduced to spectator.

Friar Bones stuck an arm out of the driver's window and dispatched the man on the other fender with two quick pistol shots. A Chechen jumped onto the opposite running board and smashed out the passenger window with a rifle butt. I had a sliver view inside the cab through the top of the back window. Muzzle flash from Friar Bones' Luger lit up the Chechen's face. The back of his head blew away into the night and he was gone. Another Chechen climbed onto the driver's running board. Friar Bones knocked him off the truck with an elbow to the head. My rifle came free and I scrambled to my feet to keep from being trampled in the melee around me.

A body blow knocked me sideways. One of the Chechens had tried to stab me. The blade of his knife had caught in Eglik's shoulder bag. He struggled to free it. This time I remembered the monk's advice and swung the toe of my rifle butt into the side of the Chechen's head. The Chechen folded down and his weight carried him over the side of the truck. One of his comrades slashed at me with a wicked looking blade about half the length of a sword. I managed to block him with the rifle. Neither of us recovered well. Drizzle had left the wood underfoot slick. The Chechen tried to close on me to use the knife. I tried to back away to get enough distance to bring my rifle to bear.

I backed right into another Chechen who looped an arm around my neck and began to choke off my air supply. I stamped ineffectually at his feet while I waved the rifle to try to fend off the other man's knife. It was a matter of not much time until they would overcome my frantic squirming. I would die with an alien stink in my nostrils, sadistic laughter in my ears and the taste of fear welling up in my mouth.

Salvation came out of nowhere.

The man with the knife jerked and jittered like a marionette and then collapsed in a heap, as if his strings had been cut. The man with his arm around my neck fell next, carrying me down. I twisted free and saw what had happened.

The stretcher case had decided to use his assault rifle. The high beams of the truck behind silhouetted a one armed man braced on the stump of a leg, firing two and three round bursts. He seemed to have a sense of who the bad guys were, but in the confusion I couldn't be sure. Maybe he knew he was going to die and wanted to take all the company with him he could. I kept a low profile until he emptied his magazine.

The instant the shooting stopped I scrambled to get my feet under me. The Chechen who had tried to strangle me was doing the same. Pain from at least one bullet wound left him clumsy and ill-balanced. I shoved him over the side of the truck.

The Chechen who had tried to stab me didn't take kindly to being shot. He was up with a roar. He charged me in a fit of rage, slashing wildly. He didn't seem to realize he had lost his knife. I sidestepped his flailing onrush and his momentum carried him over the side of the truck. Panting and spent, I looked around for my next opponent.

Only two of us were left standing on the back of the truck. The other was one of the monks. The tree had swiveled to one side of the road during the fight and the GMC made its way through a tangle of jutting branches. One of them slapped me in the face. I sat down and only the monk remained standing.

His piety was a little the worse for wear. He pried his fingers out of the knucks of a trench knife. They should have slipped easily. There was plenty of blood to lubricate them. Maybe they were just cramped from tension. He looked around his feet and shoved a dead Chechen over the side of the truck.

Once the tree was behind us, the GMC gathered a little speed. Rough ground and heavy loads held the convoy to a fast walk. Occasional gun flashes were still visible in the trees but it looked like we had broken through the Chechen lines. My best guess as to what had happened was that Gregoriev had used his remaining Spetnatz troops to mount an attack that drew the Chechens away from the roadblock. As soon as the Chechens saw that they had been suckered, they charged back to man the barricade. They had been half a step too late. I slumped against a crate.

I had no clue where Falkenberg was. Whether he was alive or dead. I was amazed at how little I cared. He was just some far off thought that flickered across my mind for no good reason. Part of a distant life I could barely remember. My immediate visceral responses revolved around physical pain and emotional torpor. I hurt almost everywhere and I was only vaguely aware of my surroundings. I felt a nudge and looked up.

The monk stood over me. "You are going to die?" he demanded, as if he wondered whether he ought to throw me overboard as well.

I started laughing.

I wasn't laughing at anything. It was just release, wild and beyond my control. It hurt my ribs but I couldn't stop. Ragged breathing syncopated it and made it sound like something leaking out of an asylum during a full moon. I just sat there howling with tears streaming down my face, knowing I had totally lost it.

"Maybe not," was all the monk had to say.

Eventually I ran out of breath and it all ended in a spasm of coughing. I was back where I started, bumping along a dirt road on a pile of crates.

"Lucky they didn't shoot out the tires," I realized, suddenly wondering why they hadn't. "Or the engine."

"No trucks, no steal," the monk said.

The age-old quest for loot. The monks had bet on greed and won. Our convoy found its way to the paved road through the pass and gained a little speed. Lights appeared in the distance. More than there should have been. I wiped the drizzle off my glasses, wondering what else was left to go wrong.

The Georgian Army had set up a check-point just outside a small village. Several truckloads of infantry were mustering beside the road. Heavy diesels rumbled to life and a main battle tank made its way down from a flatbed trailer. No more wimpy aerial strafing. The Georgian military had had enough of this proxy war shit. They had come up-country to kick ass and take names.

As a foreigner with a record of police contact, I was a prime candidate for the full treatment.

Chapter 25

An armored fighting vehicle blocked the road, silhouetted in the lights of the military activity behind it. Metal ground on metal as our convoy geared down for compression braking. Service brakes squealed and over-loaded trucks skittered to a stop. Riflemen moved to flank us on both sides. Surrounded and exhausted, I resigned myself to whatever fate held in store.

The head monk made his way to the barricade, escorted by two of his flock. The old gentleman did the talking and the officer in charge did the nodding. The armored fighting vehicle revved its diesels and backed out of our way. I stayed low among the crates while we rolled through the checkpoint.

The road wound down into the village square. An NCO stopped us there and positioned our trucks in a rank where the headlights could add illumination to a medical triage station. Lowering our half-conscious Spetnatz casualty required me to climb down the side of the truck with him to stabilize his squirming. My feet touched the ground and my legs turned to rubber. I landed on my backside.

Two monks picked up the casualty and left me staring at the triage station. A few of the injured were propped against a cistern, the others laid out on cobblestones. Probably those who had made it to the paved road and been picked up by Georgian patrols. Falkenberg wasn't among them. If he had made it this far he would be among the discarded dead. I gained my feet and launched myself toward a ragged row of covered bodies.

Two men watched over one. Erect posture made them Spetnatz troopers in spite of their peasant mufti. Only the bulk of a torso and part of a head remained under the blanket at their feet. I saw no lower limbs.

"Greg-Gregoriev?" I managed to stammer out.

"Maybe they will make him Colonel," one trooper said. "The Generals and the politicians. Now that he is gone, maybe they will make him Colonel."

"F-Falkenberg?" I asked.

The trooper let a disgusted look do his talking.

That left me shambling from body to body. They had been hastily covered. None of the protruding bits of clothing matched Falkenberg's custom tailoring. I couldn't spend time searching. As soon as the Georgian Army sorted out the confusion, bureaucracy would set in. I might never extricate myself. I moved away from the triage station before the sights and smells could take control of my stomach.

The village was a collection of crooked little streets and bungalows huddled in darkness. The occupants wanted no attention from the soldiers who had come for God knew what reason. The military had stopped two trucks and a bus below the village and were turning them around. On my last trip I traded the hash Friar Bones sold me for a ride to Tblisi. I had no trade goods but I did see Friar Bones. I went that way as fast as my wobbly legs would carry me and planted myself in front of him.

"Can you get me on that bus?" I asked.

His scary eyes were a wordless demand to know why he should. I needed inspiration. Fast.

"Scroll fragments." I patted Eglik's shoulder bag. "Scientific tests. Prove they're authentic."

No sooner had I blurted that out than I recalled Eglik's admonition that selling the Scrolls was the Church Fathers' idea. That the monks hadn't taken kindly to it. Friar Bones' silence gave the concept personality. I made him a better offer.

"Put me on that bus and you're rid of me forever."

Friar Bones seized my arm, hauled me down to where the bus was turning and hit the door with the heel of his hand. The driver opened up and peered at me. He didn't like my looks. I couldn't have paid him enough for a ride even if I'd had money and known the language. Friar Bones installed me in a front seat, put the fear of God into the driver in twenty five words or less and dismounted. The driver closed the door and got the bus underway. There were probably passengers in the seats behind me. I didn't look. I didn't care.

Time and distance lost all meaning. Lights passed occasionally and showed a vague reflection in the soiled glass beside my head. My face had no expression, my eyes no focus. I recalled reading about the thousand yard stare. Soldiers emerging from the trauma of combat stripped of emotion and reaction. The lights grew more frequent as we drew into the outskirts of Tblisi. I needed to pull myself back to reality.

"Villa Berika," I told the driver.

This was a bus, not a taxi, and there was no reason for him to go out of his way, but he pulled up in front fifteen minutes later. When Friar Bones scared them, they stayed scared. I mumbled the best Russian thanks I could manage and got out.

It seemed like eternity since I had left the hotel but in fact it wasn't yet midnight and there were still guests in the lobby. People gave me a wide berth while I waited for the elevator. No one rode up with me. I chained myself in my room and made my way into the bathroom.

The mirror gave me a start. Filth covered me from the top of my head to the bottom of the glass, a compost of dirt and smoke and soot. My hair was a collection of tangles and cowlicks. Peeling off my clothing revealed an inventory of scrapes and contusions that would have filled several autopsy forms. It took a lot of painful scrubbing before the shower ran clean. I toweled off and collapsed in a chair.

Eglik's bag lay on the carpet where I had shed it. Chechen knives had punctured and slashed it. Peeling back the side was easier than trying to force the lock. The contents that saved me were bales of cash. The loot was all foreign and may not have been worth much in American dollars but there was plenty of it. I pulled it out carefully, stack by stack, and set it aside. Nestled among the currency I found six small sealed jars, tinted yellow, probably to protect the contents against direct sunlight. I lined them up reverently on the night stand.

Inside I could make out bits of wood, leather, and parchment. I was looking at relics of the Alexandria Scrolls; history that went back sixteen centuries and possibly more. They were my responsibility now. It would be up to me to get them safely to the people who could authenticate them. It put a new kind of dread into me. I felt a profound inadequacy, a fear that I would blow the only significant opportunity that would ever come my way.

A call to the concierge got me a promise that I'd be booked on a flight as soon as Aeroflot opened in the morning. Beyond that the situation was out of my hands. Either the Georgian military would find Falkenberg or they wouldn't and either he would be alive or he wouldn't. I turned out the lights and crawled into bed.

Sleep brought nightmares. Men with torn bodies and twisted features, each demanding to know what right I had to be alive when he was dead. Headlong flight accomplished nothing. Every path I took brought me face to face with another corpse. The torment didn't end until the first light of day showed behind the drapes. Then I had to elude real pursuit.

My business suit conspired with a spreading black eye and unruly hair to give me a schizophrenic appearance but it was the best imitation of presentable I could manage. I packed rapidly and checked out. The first cab in line took me to the express office. I couldn't afford to risk losing the relics in a customs inspection. I boxed up the jars and the cash, sent them off to my home address and had the driver take me to the airport to follow them.

I used the Istanbul stop to phone Jerry Silver but it was still night in Washington so I was in London by the time I got hold of him.

"Have you heard from Alex?" I asked.

"Where the hell have you been?" he demanded.

"I need to know whether you've heard from Alex."

"Are you aware that Interpol is looking for you?"

"What for?" I tried to sound innocent.

"This Scalded Woman business."

That surprised me. "What about it?"

"Their informants said you talked to her in Tblisi."

That added injustice to injury. I couldn't get kidnapped without getting into trouble with the law.

"Well, did you?" Jerry asked.

"Are they accusing me of anything specific?"

"They know The Scalded Woman has the Scrolls."

I felt my grip on the phone tighten. "Do they have proof? Or is that just another police theory?"

He cooled down and sounded more like a juris doctor. "Well, this is a reconstruction based on the questions that Nordheim character was firing at me and the little bit of cross examination I was able to slip in, but I think it is fairly accurate, although not as precise as I would like. Interpol, as I gather, was keeping a close watch on the Scalded Woman in Tblisi. There was some sort of incident and they lost track. Nordheim made it sound like their informants were lucky to escape with their lives. Probably an exaggeration to cover their incompetence."

There was no point in telling him otherwise. Particularly not on an open international telephone line.

"By the time Interpol re-established contact," he went on, "the gang had already been to the monastery where the Scrolls were kept and left. Their convoy was across the border into Azerbaijan enroute to Iran. It took a number of high level phone calls to get the Azerbaijani police to stop the trucks. There were plenty of red faces when nothing was found."

"No Scrolls?" I asked.

"The trucks were a decoy. The gang had also chartered an old Russian cargo plane. An Antonov something or other. One of those lumbering propeller contraptions that can land on short, unimproved strips. Before Interpol discovered the ruse, the plane had been unloaded in Iran."

"So if Interpol screwed up, what do they want with me?" I asked.

"It's a short step from International Police Force to international laughing stock. They'll want a scapegoat."

"I don't think so, Jerry. My passport has been entered into customs computers in Tblisi, Istanbul and London. If Interpol wanted me, they'd have me."

I could almost hear the perplexity in his silence. "There is something you should know," he finally said. "This Eddington character Alex has been dealing with may be an impostor. Interpol has reason to believe the real Eddington is dead."

"That sounds serious," I agreed. "I'll get off your phone so you can get to work locating Alex."

My hand was trembling when I hung up. The fact that Interpol hadn't vacuumed me up yet didn't mean they weren't about to. I needed to get back on US soil where I could fight extradition.

First I had to make my connection out of London. Heathrow security was serious about terrorist threats on U.S. bound aircraft and my appearance set off alarm bells. My luggage was searched twice. I was gone over with a metal detecting wand. I was X-rayed. More time ticked away while I stood in front of a man at a computer answering endless questions. I made the flight with minutes to spare.

The plane ride to Seattle was long and uncomfortable. The aches were beginning to settle in. I felt conspicuous behind my black eye. Toward the end I just felt punk. Not even the familiar surroundings of Sea-Tac airport cheered me up. I retrieved my luggage before anyone could show up to handcuff me and grabbed the first cab in line for a queasy ride home.

My symptoms went downhill fast. First chills, then fever. I self-prescribed a dose of penicillin left over from my last root canal, washed down a hydrocodone tablet and crawled into bed where I could die in peace. The authorities would find my body when they came looking for me. I wouldn't have to answer any questions or face any consequences.

A night's sleep cleared my head. I took my symptoms to the local Doc-In-A-Box. They made a painful job of opening my two largest red spots and found staph infection chewing merrily through my flesh. They flushed out lots of goo and stuffed the holes full of antiseptic wound tape. They made me watch so I would know how to change the dressings myself. Then they punched a needle into my backside to jump start my immune system and put me on a ten day course of Cipro and Bactrim. The phone was ringing when I got home from the pharmacy.

"Owen Doran." I hoped it was news about Falkenberg.

It was Mary Ann the missionary. "Do you have the Scrolls?"

"No."

"You have to turn them over as soon as you get them."

"Mary Ann, forget the Scrolls. They--"

"If you don't, it will be just too bad for you."

"Stop trying to sound like an old gangster movie and listen to--."

"You'll receive instructions." She hung up.

Mixing a rum and coke and brooding probably wasn't what the doctor had in mind when she told me to drink fluids and get plenty of rest.

Falkenberg was missing and possibly gone for good. The Scrolls were on the fast track to the black market. I was receiving threatening phone calls from religious kooks. There was a good chance the police were closing in on me. And I had run as far as I could run. This was my last sanctuary. There was nothing to do but wait to see if the Scroll fragments arrived, or if I had screwed that up too.

Chapter 26

Overwhelmed and helpless were feelings life had given me plenty of experience with. My standard defense mechanism was to bury myself in a comfortable routine. Something I could do without compounding my failures. I turned to the grant applications that had been piling up in the Foundation's inbox.

The golden oldies were back to haunt me. There had been dinosaurs on Noah's Ark; two million dollars for an expedition to find the old tub and turn paleontology on its ear. Davey Crocket hadn't died at the Alamo. He had been imprisoned and eventually released in Mexico, where he lived to a ripe old age pumping his DNA into any senorita who would take a couple of pesos to lift her petticoats; two hundred fifty thousand for travel, testing and tequila. A Viking named Torvald the Grim had discovered the lost continent of Lemuria and left a deerskin map; five million to outfit a search vessel. I spent the remainder of that day and most of the next reviewing and politely declining those and more like them before the express truck pulled up outside.

It was the package from Tbilisi. I cleared the kitchen table, used a paring knife to slit my clumsy taping job and felt my blood turn to ice. I had been on the edge of panic when I packed the currency in the Tblisi express office, shoving it in any way I could, hoping I wouldn't be seen. The bundles I took out were neatly squared. Someone with the ability to track express packages and the authority to intercept them had opened and resealed this one. I stacked the money on one end of the table and lined up the six jars on the other.

The shipment had arrived intact. It shouldn't have. Sending bundles of undeclared foreign currency into the country was a no-no, never mind undocumented artifacts. The sense that people were watching creeped me out. The knowledge that they could close in any time gave me a new urgency. I had to deal with the artifacts now.

The Foundation contracted with a lab to validate radio-carbon dating submitted by grant holders. They were happy to do the wood and leather but didn't have the equipment to test the ink on the parchment and didn't feel comfortable recommending a lab that specialized in that work. They suggested I consult reliable members of the academic community. I called Professor Berryman instead.

"Ah, Mr. Doran," he said. "The soft copy of the Scrolls appears to have arrived intact."

"How is the translation coming?"

He cleared his throat rather than answer. "I have received disturbing information that my department's copy is not exclusive."

"I don't recall saying it would be."

"Well, I certainly thought, as Professor Eddington's superior, that I would be entitled to some consideration."

"Doctor, I don't control the Scrolls. There could be any number of copies in circulation. You received one as a courtesy. If you prefer not to participate in translation, then don't."

That shut him up. It even surprised me. Normally I wasn't that crisp. I put it down to stress and told him the foundation had recovered Scroll fragments and needed spectrographic analysis of the ink. He sounded cagey when he recommended a lab, like he was steering me someplace he could get inside information. I thanked him and hung up, wondering how smart it had been to admit to willful possession of artifacts in two successive conversations that might have been recorded under a court approved wiretap.

A web search on Berryman's recommendation told me who their competitors were and I was able to pick out the industry leader. Devious wasn't my nature, but Berryman's attitude irritated me. I had risked my life and Falkenberg might well have lost his trying to recover the Scrolls. I didn't like some academic poobah acting as if they were his personal property. I made arrangements to have the ink tested and then called Jerry Silver.

"Is there any word on Alex?" I asked.

He didn't answer right away. His silence put my nerves on edge. When he spoke, it was with exquisite elocution.

"Owen, is there something you want to tell me?"

"Like what?"

"Is there something I should know as the Foundation's attorney?"

"What are you babbling about?"

"There is a report," he said, "unofficial as yet, about a mass murder in a Georgian monastery."

"Jerry, have you located Alex? Yes or no?"

"He is hospitalized in Tblisi with gunshot and fragmentation wounds."

Better than dead was my first thought. The second came tumbling out of my mouth.

"How serious?"

"The Embassy doctor has seen him. Immediate return to the U.S. for treatment is strongly recommended."

"When do you expect him?"

"The Georgian authorities have detained him. I need the facts, Owen. I need to know where Alex stands so I can get him out."

"Forget the legal drivel. Get in touch with Alex's cronies. Call in as many favors as it takes."

Jerry wasn't taking any short answers. He knew Falkenberg's penchant for risk and he pressed for details. If the facts got out, Falkenberg might spend the rest of his life in Georgia. I stonewalled until Jerry finally hung up in frustration.

I had run out on Falkenberg. There was no getting around that. Never mind that he was the victim of his own scheme. Never mind that he had kept me in the dark from day one and put me in no end of danger. I hadn't stuck around and seen it through. I didn't know whether his cronies had enough pull to get him out of Georgia but they were his best shot. Even if they could, his medical condition was liable to keep him out of action indefinitely. That left me to extricate myself and the Foundation from whatever trouble his Scroll-hunting expedition had stirred up. I mixed a Cuba Libre and slumped into my favorite chair.

Drinking and thinking wasn't the best combination but when something did occur to me I had absorbed enough eighty proof nerve to follow up. I ransacked my luggage and located Dr. Aaron Skinner's weighty tome. I wasn't interested in the end of the world. All I wanted was a phone number.

My first contact was a machine. I selected "O" for operator. She wasn't much help but I made myself obnoxious enough that she transferred the call to a supervisor.

"How may I help you, Sir?" A smooth voice full of concern.

"My name is Owen Doran." I spelled it for him. "Tell Skinner I record my phone calls. I want to talk to him about the one I received from a member of his staff. Either that or the tape goes to the FBI."

"I'm sorry, Sir. There must be some mistake. In any event, Dr. Skinner is not available at present."

"Skinner is available. This is the twenty first century. He's a cell phone call away."

"Sir, I cannot--"

"If I wanted to talk to a moron, I wouldn't have wasted long distance charges. We have plenty of them in this area code. Call Skinner."

"Hold, please," the voice said.

I started sweating. The call was an inspiration born of liquor and I hadn't thought about what I would say if I got through to the man himself.

"This is Dr. Aaron Skinner, Mr. Doran."

I could practically hear the fire and brimstone looking for a way out from behind the silken veneer.

"I'll be brief, Doctor. Your girl Mary Ann called me. I don't have the Alexandria Scrolls and I don't like being threatened."

"The Scrolls are a tool of the Anti-Christ. They must be destroyed."

"They are black market gold and the authorities know it. It's a good bet they have tapped this phone."

"That does not concern me, Mr. Doran. I have committed no overt act. I have no criminal intent. My only interest in the Scrolls arises from legitimate spiritual concerns. Mary Ann is an unfortunate child raised by a disturbed mother in a series of seedy trailer courts. I took her into my flock in the hope of shielding her from a life of sin. If I have failed I am saddened but not surprised."

He cut the connection.

On the surface it was a neat little speech. He had just read a statement exonerating himself into the official record of whatever investigation might be going on. Like most stuffed shirts, he was a sucker for any opportunity to run his mouth. The fact that he took my call confirmed that he was behind the Evangelicals hunting the Scrolls. They weren't just renegades hiding behind his name. And that he was still serious about getting his hands on them. I dug through the business cards in my desk and made another call.

"This is Barbara Wren."

No machine. She probably had caller ID. She had answered in person because she knew who it was and wanted to know what I knew.

"Owen Doran, Barbara," I said. "I hope you don't mind my calling you Barbara."

"How was your trip?" All business.

"Not as bad as Alex Falkenberg's."

"Poor Alex. Is there any news?"

"We didn't get the Scrolls," I told her. "But we did recover some datable material associated with them. Artifacts that may help establish their age."

"That could be useful," she said in a voice that encouraged me to drop any other tidbits I might have. "How is the translation coming?"

"I'll be happy to discuss it with you in detail," I said. "Will your schedule have you in Seattle any time soon."

"I'm afraid not," she replied. "You will keep me posted?"

"As soon as I have any word."

"Thank you so much for calling." She hung up.

She had made the one glaring mistake that told me what I wanted to learn from the call. She hadn't asked if I knew where the Scrolls were. The only people who wouldn't ask were people who already knew. I had no doubt how she had come by the information.

Bringing hundreds of millions of dollars worth of anything to market required preparation. I knew from a big buck car auction I had attended with Falkenberg that there was more to bidding wars than rich people wiggling their fingers. Contacts had to be made. Bank letters of credit obtained. Things that took months to do and couldn't be left to amateurs. That was Barbara's line of work. The Scalded Woman would need Barbara and probably more like her to line up the players who could pay top dollar for the Scrolls.

Seattle was a day trip from San Francisco, and with its concentration of high-tech fortunes, was the first place anyone would look for buyers of anything exotic and expensive. I decided Barbara had already planned that trip and didn't want me to know about it.

Aside from my lack of savoir-faire, there was another reason she might want to keep her distance. The Scalded Woman might be using the Falkenberg Foundation as a lightning rod to draw law enforcement attention while she spirited the Scrolls into the country. Which meant I now confronted an organization of ruthless smugglers; the Reverend Doctor Aaron Skinner, complete with an entourage of one temptress and an uncertain count of mighty men; and Interpol, probably in cahoots with no end of U.S. Federal, State and Local law enforcement agencies.

Driving to the Post Office to register and ship the six jars of relics from the monastery, I recalled Friar Bones' advice. Only a fool confronts his adversary. Sneak up on him. Shoot him from behind. Never brag about it. I couldn't sneak up on that many people at once, and I couldn't shoot them even if I managed it, but the idea wouldn't stop nagging at me. Gradually it grew into the beginnings of a plan.

Chapter 27

King County Airport was the catch basin of Puget Sound aviation. Built in the nineteen twenties when Trimotor Fords flew the mail, it reigned for a quarter century as the region's premier air terminal. Now it hunkered in the industrial flatland of South Seattle under the flight path of Seattle-Tacoma International; a dawn to dusk bustle of corporate and cargo jets, charter flights, bottom tier commuters and private aircraft. I drove in as tense as I was the day I arrived for my first flying lesson.

That had been two years ago, right after Falkenberg and his cronies had sold the company. Flush with the first real success I had ever tasted, I forgot that I was a panic-prone nerd with a fear of heights. Once I started something, I was too stubborn to give up, no matter how big a fool I made of myself. Sixty five hours of white knuckles and patient instruction later, I had a license. My Honda remembered the way to the flight school and they were happy to take my money to rent one of their aging Cessnas. I went through the pre-flight and start-up procedure hoping the familiar routine would settle my nerves.

Brisk wind had blown the morning mist out of the sky and left only a few billows of cloud. I taxied to the run-up area, went through the checklist and switched to the control tower radio frequency to announce my intentions.

"Cleared for take-off," the tower came back. "Straight out departure approved."

I lined up the Cessna on the short runway, did a final instrument check and applied full power. Fifty-five knot rotation speed came up quickly. The wheels lifted free of the tarmac. The adrenaline rush of flying kicked in as I began my climb to altitude. Step one of my plan was complete. The

FAA, and by extension the rest of the Federal Government, knew which way I was headed. Step two began five miles out over Puget Sound. I switched the radio frequency to Seattle Departure and gave the controller my aircraft number.

"Request flight following," I said.

Flight following was a radar service that provided separation advisory for small aircraft under visual flight rules. It was available only when the air traffic control system had some slack time from managing large jets and commuter aircraft. This close to Seattle, with three major airfields inside a twenty mile radius, that was never.

"Flight following approved," the controller came back. "Squak four two niner one."

The transponder digits she gave me would mark my aircraft on her radar screen. That left no doubt the government had an interest in my movements.

"Roche Harbor," I said in response to her question about my destination.

It was a forty minute flight over the San Juan Archipelago, islands of greenery and granite jutting out of the white capped expanse of the Sound, unspoiled retreats for the rich and the off-beat. San Juan Island was the largest, fifty odd square miles of pastureland surrounded by seventy five miles of secluded coast. A single ferry dock, a couple of resort towns and whale-watchers too ga-ga over endangered species to notice anything else. Roche Harbor lay at the north end of the Island, just this side of the Canadian border. You couldn't find a better place to land contraband. I focused on landing the Cessna.

There was private airstrip on the heights above the harbor. You wouldn't have seen it if you didn't know where to look. It was that narrow and secluded. Wind gusts off the Strait of Juan de Fuca gave me a rough ride on the way down. Tall evergreens rose up on either side, a none-too-subtle hint of what could happen if I didn't touch down precisely on the slim ribbon of asphalt. As soon as I had the wheels rolling straight on the tarmac I reconfigured the plane, brought the engine to full power and took off.

Mission accomplished. I had marked the site on Federal radar. Literally. At first it felt like victory. Then I wasn't so sure. On the flight back to King County I began having second thoughts about my brilliant scheme.

It was something I had ginned up on fitful sleep and unpredictable medication. The idea had come to me while I was thinking over the situation in Georgia. Originally I had seen the Orthodox Church as a victim. Beset by American Evangelists. Forced to sell their treasures on the black market. Pawns in a Russian military operation. It took me a while to figure out that they were the only players in the game who couldn't lose.

The Russians oppressing their country and the Chechens opposing their religion would kill each other off. The Church not only would get paid for Scrolls they had already copied but would be spared the ongoing expense of conservatorship. As soon as the gas cleared out of the Monastery, the monks could move back in. A text book case of a patsy turning the tables. In a stunning burst of hubris, I had extrapolated their success to my own situation and come up with a plan to set my tormentors against each other.

Stupid didn't begin to describe the comparison. The Georgian Orthodox Church was operating in a country where they were the highest moral authority. They had organization, public support and probably no small amount of legal and de-facto immunity. I was a four-eyed bean counter in a land where only celebrities were revered and not even they were immune.

The situation deteriorated when I turned in the Cessna and went out to retrieve my Honda. Someone had duct-taped a disposable cell phone to the outside of the drivers' window. The attached note had come from a laser printer.

Don't call us. We'll call you.

I drove home with one eye on the mirror. If anyone followed me, I didn't see them.

The first order of business was redressing my staph infection. The pads under the bandages were liberally soaked with blood and pus. Pulling them loose was no fun. Next up was using tweezers to tease sodden wound tape out of the holes in my flesh. It didn't come easily or painlessly. Gritting my teeth got me through the antiseptic flush. Then it was push in fresh tape and balance fresh pads while I did my best to wrap them down with self-adhesive bandages. The mess I had to clear away would have done credit to an ER after a four car pile-up. I mixed a rum and coke feeling small and vulnerable and sorry for myself.

There was no way to know whether Falkenberg ever had private misgivings about his loopy schemes. Or whether Gregoriev had second thoughts about the plan to destroy the Chechen forces in Georgia. The consequences were clear. Gregoriev the guest of honor at a closed-coffin funeral. Falkenberg languishing in a foreign hospital. I called Barbara Wren before the last of my nerve evaporated.

"Owen," she said with just the right touch of polite enthusiasm, "I hadn't expected to hear from you so soon."

I hadn't expected to choke at the sound of her voice. It was a chilling reminder that my social skills were not in her league and that I was almost certain to strike out. I mustered what voice I could and pushed on anyway.

"I'd like to have dinner with you this Saturday."

Not exactly suave, but it got the message across. I gave her the name of the resort at Roche Harbor, pronouncing it carefully so anyone monitoring the call would be sure to get it, and the time for which I had reserved a table. She let out a surprised laugh.

"I don't think I'll be able to--"

"I know this is all very sudden and we're not that well acquainted, so why don't you bring Sofia along as a chaperone."

Her voice lost none of its politeness but all of its enthusiasm. "I have no plans to be in the Seattle area."

"Oh, come on. It's a quick trip. You'll enjoy the change of scenery, and I think I can make it worth your while."

"Can you be more specific?"

"I'd be happy to. On Saturday."

I hung up.

I had zero experience conning people, particularly not women as sophisticated as Barbara Wren, and I had probably screwed it up in ways I couldn't begin to imagine. Since I had no way to contact Sofia, I had to rely on my hunch that they were at least in touch with each other. Not that there was any reason either woman should come. I was taking a chance they would want to find out what, if anything, I knew about the Scrolls. The more I thought about it, the less likely it seemed.

The disposable cell phone went off that afternoon.

"Owen Doran."

"It's me." Mary Ann again.

"I think you and I should have dinner on Saturday," I said. "I really enjoyed dessert last time."

"You have to turn over the Scrolls," she insisted.

"We can talk about that, too."

I described the Island and the resort and gave her the same time Saturday that I'd given Barbara Wren.

"You'll have the Scrolls there?"

"I'll be prepared to talk about them."

There was silence and I thought I could hear a muffled conference. Finally she came back on.

"All right," she cooed, sounding like a b-movie version of Salome just before she did the hootchie kootchie for John the Baptist. "I'll see you then."

The trap was set. The Federal Agents monitoring my every move would stake out the resort. The worst that would happen would be me leering at some cleavage across a dinner table but the Feds would have to assume critical information was passed and they would start following the real culprits, eventually losing interest in me and the Foundation. It sounded moronic. I put the cell phone in a vise in the garage and made sure it would never ring again.

My next call was from Jerry Silver.

"Alex will be back in the country on Sunday," he announced with no small amount of pride.

I hoped I would still be out of custody then. "What kind of shape is he in?"

"Shattered hip. Numerous fragmentation wounds. Persistent infection. His doctors will be standing by to make an evaluation as soon as he arrives at the hospital."

"You might want to find him some security," I said.

"Security? Against what?"

"There are some Evangelical Christians looking for the Scrolls. They've threatened me and they may do the same with Alex, if they think he is vulnerable."

I gave Jerry, and anyone listening in, the names of the two people in Skinner's organization I knew. He promised to have somebody on Falkenberg's hospital room door twenty four seven. I hung up, dug out the Luger and loaded it.

Skinner's Mighty Men might decide to forego the pleasantries and deal with me as they had Eddington. The Scalded Woman might not like my being anything but a cooperative patsy and decide to take me out before I could make any trouble. I holed up until Saturday afternoon, working on Foundation business and trying not to dwell on what a fool I was about to make of myself.

Taking the Luger was out of the question. A concealed weapon could land me in jail. Dressing for an informal dinner was nothing unusual but this time it left me feeling as out of place as a school boy washing behind his ears to get ready for the prom. The Cessna was fueled and ready when I got to the airfield. The weather was perfect for flying. It was only vacation schedules that went wrong. Brainless stunts came off like clockwork. I arrived over Roche Harbor exactly on time.

Dusk wasn't conducive to depth perception but my bumpy landing probably had more to do with nerves. I tied down the plane and tucked my ten dollar landing fee in the drop box. Roche Harbor was more village than town and nothing was very far from anything else. It was a crisp autumn evening and I had the pedestrian walkway down to McMillin's to myself.

Mr. McMillin, according to a thumbnail history in the brochure, once operated the largest lime mine and cement factory west of the Mississippi on San Juan Island. During the decades following his death mining petered out and tourists began to trickle in. The harbor became a marina. McMillin's former mansion was moved on rollers to the top of a rise to serve as a hostel. A restaurant bearing his name had been built next to the marina.

The hostess seated me beside windows set to catch the last colors of sunset. I caught my reflection. Owen Doran, tomb raider. A pathetic bean counter done up in a sport coat and an open collar dress shirt. I wondered how long they would let me sit there alone before they kicked me out.

A float plane touched down in the harbor, taxied to a lighted pier and replaced my funk with panic. Sofia had finagled a ride in the co-pilot's seat. Barbara Wren alit from the rear. The hostess chose that minute to arrive with Mary Ann.

Chapter 28

Mary Ann's seductress outfit screamed outlet store; tight white toreador pants, a red sash and a burgundy blouse with an acre of ruffles in front, open low enough to suggest that she could be coaxed out of it. Her hairdo was a Hollywood wave, her lipstick a neon shade of carmine. Her smile reminded me of the teeth-whitening commercials on TV. Since I had appointed myself host and gentleman for the evening, I stood anyway.

"Good evening," I said. "And don't you look lovely tonight?"

The hostess held a chair and asked if she could start us off with a beverage. Mary Ann sat down beaming. I shook my head.

"Give us a few minutes, please. The rest of our party just arrived on the float plane."

The hostess smiled and left. Confusion robbed Mary Ann of words. I winked at her and sat down.

"The other women," I said. "You knew there would be more than one, didn't you?"

She drew herself up, eyes brimming with indignation. This was to have been her moment. She was all the bad girls of the Bible rolled into one. Jezebel luring. Salome dancing. Delilah snipping. Her jaw sagged when she got a look at the real deal.

The hostess guided Barbara and Sofia through the maze of tables crowding the dining area. Barbara moved with a ballroom grace that made woolen slacks and a cashmere hoodie look like haute couture. A fashionable jump suit did its best to de-emphasize Sofia's assets. Neither woman flashed skin or jewelry but there wasn't a man in the place who didn't feel the heat. I stood to hold a chair for Sofia while the hostess seated Barbara.

"May I start you off with a beverage?" the hostess asked again.

"Tea, please," Barbara said. "Earl Grey, if you have it."

"Yes, ma'am."

"Do you have something in Pekoe?" Sofia asked in her softly accented contralto.

"Yes, ma'am."

It was Mary Ann's turn. "Coffee, please."

No 'yes ma'am' for her. I told the hostess I was fine with water. I had resolved to keep a clear head. I had been thinking only of liquor. I hadn't counted on the prevailing estrogen level.

Clear head or not, one thing was obvious. My clumsy little dinner party had happened because it suited the purposes of powerful people to make it happen, and for no other reason. Those people were not likely to have the best interests of Owen Doran in mind.

"Well," I said, trying to cover my nerves with a hearty voice, "I guess introductions are in order."

Since I hadn't requested one of the premier view tables, I suspected that Federal Law Enforcement had picked our accommodations because the adjacent windows offered the best angle for their surveillance cameras. I hoped there were microphones to record any conversation I might be able to strike up.

"Mary Ann," I said, beginning with my most likely prospect, "this is Barbara Wren. Her late husband was an associate of Professor Eddington."

Mary Ann stiffened. "The Anti-Christ."

Not even Barbara was sophisticated enough to cover her surprise at that. I gave Mary Ann my best imitation of a curious smile.

"Didn't you say something about Doctor Skinner's Mighty Men slaying Eddington?"

"They slew him as Goliath was slain." Her voice fell to a fearful hush. "But he is risen."

Barbara shot me a worried glance.

"The Reverend Doctor Skinner," I explained, "is an evangelist who would like to get his hands on the Scrolls. Mary Ann is one of his disciples."

Barbara said nothing. Sofia certainly remembered Mary Ann from the Villa Berika but betrayed no recognition. They were professionals. I would have to use some imagination if I wanted to get anything out of them.

Before I could muster any bright ideas, a waiter arrived with beverages and menus and began chattering about the specials.

Barbara was intrigued by the salmon and very particular about how she wanted hers prepared. Mary Ann was shrewd enough to ask for the same. Her ploy didn't cover the fact that she was clueless trailer trash but it spared excessive embarrassment. Sofia went with a shellfish entrée. Since she could probably out-cook the entire kitchen staff, I decided it was the best bet on the menu.

"Okay, ladies," I piped up as soon as the waiter left, "just so we're all on the same page, let's go over what brought us here."

If Barbara and Sofia weren't going to say anything, then I would read my version into the Federal record and put them in a position where they could either deny it or let it stand.

"This all started with well-financed American Evangelicals scouring poor countries for converts. Local religions need money to respond. In Georgia, the Orthodox Church decided to sell one of its treasures; the so-called Alexandria Scrolls. It might well be the deal of the century. Everyone wants a piece. First up, dissolute professor and part-time relic scavenger Roald Eddington."

I winked at Barbara. She didn't speak but she was attentive, as if at least part of what she was hearing was new information.

"Eddington convinced the Church fathers that he could sucker the Falkenberg Foundation into translating and authenticating the Scrolls to support eventual sale in the lucrative U.S. market. Somewhere in the process, Evangelicals in the person of an unscrupulous pulpit-pounder who calls himself the Reverend Doctor Aaron Skinner, got wind of the deal."

I paused to give Mary Ann a chance to say something emphatic for the Feds. Not a peep. She was learning from her dinner companions. I pushed on.

"Skinner hired an ex-soldier named Lew Manders to raid the monastery where the Scrolls were kept. Eddington warned the monks. Manders' raid ended in disaster. Both Manders and Eddington were subsequently murdered. Sofia, your associates won the right to auction the Scrolls. Barbara, you are lining up prospective bidders."

Barbara took a delicate sip of her tea. "What you are saying is that potential income from auction brought the Scrolls to light."

"That seems to be the consensus."

"Then without such an auction," she asked, "mightn't the Church have elected to sell icons or statues or something such instead? Wouldn't history of incalculable value have been left to rot away to nothing over the next few centuries?"

It was the standard tomb robbers' alibi but in this case it had a disturbing ring of truth. The waiter arrived and spared me the discomfort of responding. Mary Ann let Barbara start so she would know which fork to use on her salad. Sofia and I received chowder.

"So, Owen, why have you invited us here?" Sofia asked.

A better question would have been why they came. I didn't think I'd get a straight answer, so rather than ask I took advantage of Sofia's opening to memorialize my position on the Federal record.

"Well, you know, I don't like to complain but there does come a time when enough is enough. My interest in the Alexandria Scrolls is solely as a representative of the Falkenberg Foundation. We want only to authenticate the Scrolls, have a digital copy translated and place the contents in the public domain. We make no money from the recovery, transport or sale of the actual Scrolls. So I invited you all to dinner as representatives of your various interests to ask if you would please exclude the Foundation from your activities."

Barbara patted her lips with a napkin. "If there is to be an auction, as you suggest, aren't authentication and translation necessary to establish the value of the Scrolls?"

Sofia's tone was more solemn. "You can't pick and chose what you want from life, Owen. You must take the bad with the good."

The waiter came back with some of the good. He collected dishes and dealt entrees from a tray with the dexterity of a card sharp, garnishing to taste. Barbara and Sofia were pictures of feminine delicacy during the process. Mary Ann grew increasingly tense. As soon as the waiter was gone, she spoke in a low, taut voice.

"The Scrolls are a tool of the Anti-Christ. They must be destroyed."

Barbara considered her with polite curiosity. "Have you read *Revelation*?"

"Yes."

"By yourself?" Barbara asked. "Without a Bible study teacher telling you what to think of it?"

"Yes." Vehemence made the word an obvious lie.

Barbara nibbled on a bite of salmon. "Then you remember that your Anti-Christ—I believe *Revelation* calls him Devil, Adversary or False Prophet—was set loose by the messenger of the Lord to gather together all the unbelievers."

"The Anti-Christ is the enemy of God."

"Do you have your Bible with you?" Barbara asked.

"You're one of them!"

Barbara smile and shook her head. I got the impression that she wasn't just dallying with intellectual argument. She cared enough to warn Mary Ann away from something foolish and potentially dangerous. Mary Ann was in no mood to be patronized. She turned on me.

"You said she was one of them!"

"What I said was that if *Revelation* were the prophecy you people claim it to be, then the future was set in stone and none of us could influence it."

"You're twisting the Word of God," Mary Ann warned.

"That's Skinner's forte," I said.

"Religious men," Sofia put in, "speak only what profits them and makes grander their houses of worship."

"You're all part of it," she said, looking from one of us to the other. "You're all disciples of the Anti-Christ."

She spilled her chair standing up, backed away from the table and then turned and rushed out of the dining room. The scene attracted gawkers. Barbara and Sofia were accustomed to being stared at. I followed their example and just went on with my dinner.

The conversation was by then out of my hands. Barbara was all charm and sophistication, adept at steering discussion. She chatted about cathedrals in Paris and the Metropolitan Museum of Art. Sofia added color with descriptions of the places she had visited. It was my first unfiltered insight into the things they enjoyed, and it turned dinner into something more personal and pleasant than I had planned. There was no sign of the float plane when we finished, so I asked the ladies if I could walk them to whatever transportation they had arranged.

Sofia shook her head. "We must go alone."

She put on a headscarf as we stepped outside. Barbara raised her cashmere hood. Normally I would have attributed that to the chill night air but things began to dawn on me. Both women wore flat heeled shoes. No dresses. No purses. They had come prepared to move fast if they had to. We were alone on the walkway. The ocean breeze made mysterious noises in the shrubbery of an adjoining garden. The crowd in the building seemed miles away. Instinct warned me to thank my companions for a lovely evening and make myself scarce. I was a little late.

Two huskies materialized out of the darkness.

From behind a cold voice said, "No trouble. This piece has a silencer. Nobody would hear shit."

The voice triggered an unpleasant flashback to the Villa Berika. Rick Judson had returned from his ride in the laundry hamper. He sounded like a man with a score to settle. I stood perfectly still and wondered what it would feel like to be shot.

Chapter 29

Neither of Judson's soldiers looked particularly Christian. One was in his early twenties, tall and thick through the waist, with a mat of blond hair curling out from under a baseball cap and shirt tails hanging down over sagging cargo shorts. The other looked to be around forty, hunched and heavily muscled. His jeans, sweatshirt and stocking cap were veterans of outdoor labor. Cagey eyes suggested a life of hard use and little reward. I felt Judson move in close behind me.

"Okay," he said. "We take a little stroll. Nice and peaceful. Like we're all friends."

The younger husky caught Sofia's left hand and pulled her into a come-along hold that made the two of them look like a wedding usher escorting a dowager. The older man took Barbara. No arm for Owen. I felt the muzzle of Judson's gun against my spine.

"Move," he said. "Cool and slow."

We went through the garden. Wind-harried vegetation cast fidgeting shadows in the lights of the marina and of the hostel on the hill above. The restaurant's deck and gazebo were deserted. There was no one to see us pass. A van waited in the marina parking lot. I got a glimpse of Mary Ann at the wheel.

Judson caught my collar and propelled me toward the open side door. The middle row of seats had been folded into the floor and I landed there. Barbara and Sofia landed more or less on top of me. The vehicle bounced as the Judson and his crew piled in. Darkness deepened and the door clicked shut. The van got underway. I couldn't see Judson but I could hear him in the front passenger seat, talking to Mary Ann.

"Okay. Listen up. We swept this shit-box while you were inside. You know what a bait job is?"

"No," she said.

"It's a ride the cops have tricked out to catch car clouters. GPS. Transponder. Ignition disconnect. They can track us anywhere and shut us down any time they want."

A tire bumped a curb and we swerved.

"Don't panic," Judson said.

"I'm not," Mary Ann snapped.

The tension in her voice scared Judson into a more conciliatory tone. "Just listen. This is simple. There are only three roads in this burg. They make a big circle back to the marina. Plenty of trees. Lots of cover. The cops won't see shit. We bail and you keep driving. It will look normal on GPS. Take the van back to the rental place. Keys in the slot. Catch a ferry in the morning. Understand?"

"Yes."

"Any trouble with the cops," Judson went on, "ID yourself and tell them you want a lawyer. Call the number on that card I gave you. Got it?"

"Yes."

"Just keep shut until the lawyer gets there. Let him do the talking."

Mary Ann's only reply was the rush of velocity.

Mine was a rush of panic. I hadn't thought ahead to the possible outcome of a confrontation between the Feds and Judson's crew. I imagined hordes of police closing in from all sides. I even had a vision of one of them testifying at my inquest.

"I didn't want to shoot, your honor, but I saw his eyelid flicker."

I tried to worm out from under Barbara and Sofia. A foot made weight on my shoulder.

"Keep your fucking head down."

Both women were tense but neither moved. A residue of Presbyterian guilt tried to tell me their fate was my fault, the result of my moronic plan. A lifetime in the back of the bus reminded me that no one wasted time on Owen Doran unless it suited their purposes. In particular, not two women like Barbara and Sofia.

Beyond some feminine knee-jerk at being manhandled, neither had put up any resistance. Sofia's background suggested she wouldn't submit to abduction without a fight. Barbara wasn't as physical, but she had a habit of letting men know she expected to be treated like a lady. Both had seen this coming and had deliberately walked into their own kidnapping.

"All right," Judson said over his shoulder, "we get out fast. After that everything is nice and peaceful. Just like we're out for a stroll to look at the boats."

The van lurched to a stop. The door slid open. A hand grabbed the back of my collar, lifted me and thrust me out. I made one of my usual undignified landings and scrambled to get my feet under me.

Judson grabbed my arm. The van pulled away and took the Feds' high tech surveillance with it. We were right back where we started and law enforcement was off on a wild goose chase.

"Nice and casual," Judson said. "No talking."

The younger of Judson's crew led the way through the garden to the shore where the long guest pier stretched out into the marina. Barbara and Sofia followed and I followed them, with the older husky close enough behind for me to smell the fish he had for dinner. Judson and his gun brought up the rear.

Quaint Victorian lights lit the entry to the pier, in full view of the restaurant. The fact that Judson and his knuckle-draggers had to get us past witnesses was probably the only reason we weren't trussed up with duct tape. Beyond the marina lay the emptiness of Puget Sound. If they got us aboard a boat and out there, they could do whatever they wanted. We started out along the pier, past slips where kayaks sloshed gently on the tide. The wood underfoot was damp and I slipped.

The husky behind me caught my arm before I could fall. A glance told me why I was the only one with footing issues. Everyone else was wearing deck shoes. Which meant everyone else had expected a boating excursion. As usual, only Owen hadn't received the e-mail. The husky kept his grip on my arm as we continued along. I would have no chance to jump into the water.

There were lights in the marina office and on the fuel dock. They were one pier over but they might as well have been on the moon. There was no one on the guest pier. Just voices from inside a few shut-up boat cabins and an occasional burst of moronic laughter. Boating on Puget Sound consumed as much liquor as it did gasoline. I was walking my last mile to a chorus of idiots and getting desperate.

The lead husky slowed. "Where's the fucking Sea-Ray?"

"Where the pier jogs left," Judson said.

"I don't see it," the man said. His pace slowed to a cautious waddle and he peered ahead. "The slip looks empty."

There was a space between two boats, about the size a third might have made. As we drew closer, lights down low on the pier showed a radar antenna just above the water.

"Crap!" Judson said. "It sank."

"Where's Larry?"

My guess was that the boat had help going down, and anyone left to watch it had gone down with it. That meant I was trapped alone between Sofia's gang and Judson's, with no Friar Bones to help me out. Not that Friar Bones had ever done anything but hand me a gun and let me do my own fighting. The sole difference between us was attitude. He grabbed any situation by the throat, no matter how prohibitive the odds against him. That lesson was all the help I ever had received or ever would receive from him.

The pier was narrow and Judson had to shoulder his way between me and his husky to get a closer look. The husky had to let go of my arm to let Judson pass. It was an opportunity that wouldn't last. Judson was the one with the gun, so he was the one I put my shoulder against and shoved for all I was worth.

Judson went overboard cursing, grazed the prow of a moored boat and went in with a dull splash. Before I could take off running, a powerful engine cranked once and caught. The exhaust drew everyone's attention to the far end of the pier. Sofia kicked the younger husky in the back of the knee. His leg buckled. She and Barbara shoved him overboard and they made a run for the noise of the engine. The remaining husky dragged an automatic out of his pocket. I kicked his ankle and made a slippery sprint for shore.

It was dumb-ass desperation. I was silhouetted in the Victorian lights. Likely as not I would be shot dead at the next step. No one fired. No sound carried above the engine. I risked a glance back.

A stranger stood in the light at the far end of the pier holding a heavy assault rifle. He wasn't pointing it at anyone but he hefted it like he knew how to use it. Judson's husky let his pistol drop to the pier. Barbara and Sofia scrambled over the end of the pier and the rifleman followed. I was in the parking lot before I looked back to see the boat pulling away.

It was long and sleek and the air shook from the thunder of its exhaust. It picked up speed toward the mouth of the marina. Floodlights appeared out on the Sound, one on either side of a small island beyond the marina.

A pair of Coast Guard patrol boats converged toward the mouth of the marina to intercept the speedboat; big twin outboard engines in back and twin machine guns up front.

"Better late than never," I thought aloud.

Wrong again.

A heavy machine gun opened slow automatic fire from the front of the speedboat. In order to return fire, the Coast Guard would have to shoot into a marina full of boats, some with people in them. They had to pull back quickly out of range and let the speedboat into open water where they could pursue it and fire safely.

From behind me, up the hill, came the whine of a turbine. Lights came on, bright enough to banish the night. Wind rose to gale force as a Blackhawk helicopter lifted in hover and swooped out across the marina. It passed directly over me. I could see the snout of a six-barreled mini-gun protruding from one door as it swept off in pursuit of the speedboat.

Heads popped out of boats and people came out of the restaurant to watch. Blue law-enforcement strobes converged on the marina lot. Police in tactical gear hustled me out of their way and charged out along both piers, brandishing an assortment of firearms.

I had returned to my accustomed role. Owen Doran, discarded dork. I made my way up to the airfield. The Cessna was exactly as I had left it. It had probably been searched. The FAA had the authority to ramp check any aircraft any time for any reason. Or no reason. My hands were trembling when I fired the engine. I took off without the usual courtesy radio announcements.

Once I was airborne I could see the activity in the marina. Blue and red strobes flickered all along the shore. More strobes flashed on the water as patrol boats moved in through the marina. Floodlights illuminated everything. To the North I saw nothing. No sign of the speedboat, the two patrol boats or the helicopter. I turned south for the forty minute flight back to King County.

The tower didn't seem to be expecting me when I called for landing clearance. There were no police cars waiting for me when I taxied to parking. It was all way too normal. The law was certain to want to talk to me, and probably more than that. My best guess was that tonight they had focused all their resources on recovering the Scrolls and rounding up the bad guys. I drove home taking no comfort in the knowledge that they always knew where to find me.

Too wired to sleep, I mixed a drink and sat in the dark with visions of tactical squads surrounding the house and shouting through a bullhorn for me to come out with my hands up. I didn't know what I would say. The events in Roche Harbor were a blur and I had no idea what purpose they had served.

Chapter 30

Rain rode on gale-force gusts off the Pacific Ocean, white-capped and heaving beneath a menacing overcast, and clawed at the windows of Falkenberg's beach house. The cavernous living room offered sanctuary not only from nature but also from time and progress. The beamed ceiling, exotic hardwoods and expanse of Persian carpet belonged to an era when wealth bought power and privilege, no questions asked. An era Falkenberg would resurrect if he could. Which made me wonder why the nine of us were sitting there.

The fact that Falkenberg was confined to a wheel chair didn't diminish the considerable influence his money could buy even today. The chair was sleek and motorized and probably cost as much as a small car. An extension supported his left leg, sticking out straight in a full length cast. He used the controls to maneuver the chair a foot or so, just enough to demonstrate that he was its master, not its prisoner.

"Thank you all," he said to the assembled group, "for making the trip here."

Jerry Silver, State Department Attorney Rosalinda Baca and Inspector Nordheim of Interpol had flown from D.C., although not on the same plane. Jerry hovered at Falkenberg's shoulder. The two officials sat stone-faced at either end of one of the room's teak-accented sofas.

Mary Ann sat on the other in a skirt and blouse selected by someone who knew how to create an aura of innocence and vulnerability. The woman beside her hadn't been introduced. She had removed Mary Ann's handcuffs only after Rosalinda Baca had seconded Falkenberg's request.

Barbara Wren had driven up from San Francisco. She was smartly turned out in a tailored business suit and looked perfectly at home in one of Falkenberg's elegant gondola chairs. Two weeks had passed since our adventure in Roche Harbor. I had no idea what had befallen her or Sofia, or where either woman stood with the law.

Sofia had resumed residence with Falkenberg. She occupied a second gondola chair, more casually dressed in a turtleneck and slacks, keeping a hostess' eye on her guests. I occupied the third, sitting straight and trying to live up to image created by my buttoned-down shirt, silk tie and pin-striped suit.

Jerry Silver cleared his throat. "Mr. Falkenberg has been kind enough to interrupt his convalescence and open his home to clear up certain questions regarding--"

"This is an official inquiry," Rosalinda Baca snapped. "The venue resulted solely from affidavits to the effect that Mr. Falkenberg was not medically fit to travel."

Falkenberg raised a hand before Jerry could start an argument. I was sure it had taken more than paperwork to bring two bureaucrats three thousand miles. Falkenberg was up to something, but this wasn't my party and my attendance wasn't optional. All I could do was wait and see what happened.

"Please proceed," Falkenberg said.

Rosalinda Baca shot a knowing glance at Falkenberg's immobilized leg. "You are aware that it is illegal for U.S. citizens to fight in the service of any foreign power?"

"I don't recall giving the subject any thought," Falkenberg said.

She gave him a withering glare. When he didn't react, she turned it on me.

"And you, Mr. Doran?"

"I have no military experience. No training. Poor eyesight. Passive personality. I'm in sorry physical condition. No army would have any use for me."

We were following a script, of course. Jerry had laid it all out for us, dithering over the smallest details. He was even specific about how to ad-lib. Evasive answers. Change the subject. Never lie. If you're pinned down by a direct question, say you don't remember. It was standard lawyer stuff and Rosalinda Baca paid no attention.

"Inspector Nordheim," she said.

He opened a folder on his lap and found his place with a thick finger. "Mr. Falkenberg, you and Mr. Doran contacted a contingent of Russian

Special Forces troops occupying a dig site your foundation sponsors in the Georgian Republic."

Falkenberg raised his eyebrows in my direction. "Owen, are we sponsoring any activities in the Georgian Republic?"

"The Foundation has received a preliminary funding application for archaeological exploration in the region. No decision has been made. No funds advanced. No sponsorship extended."

"Well, there you have it," Falkenberg said. "Mr. Doran is the Foundation's Chief Financial Officer. If any sponsorship existed, he would know about it."

Sponsorship wasn't the issue and Nordheim ignored the exchange. "You went in company with the Russian military and a black market antiquities dealer named Sebastian Eglik to a monastery near the site."

I arched my eyebrows at Jerry. "Didn't Inspector Nordheim tell us that Sebastian Eglik was murdered some months ago in Istanbul?"

"I distinctly remember him saying that," Jerry crowed. "And both my original and transcribed notes from the interview reflect that fact."

Falkenberg had limited patience for splitting hairs. "Ms. Baca, if you had evidence, Mr. Doran and I would be in Federal custody. Your superiors didn't send you and Inspector Nordheim across the country to discuss foreign embarrassments. Nor would such a discussion require as broad an audience as you have summoned here. Why don't you tell us what you really want? We may be prepared to assist you without being bullied into it."

Rosalinda Baca also hadn't come across the country to be patronized. She had come to vanquish and dominate. She glowered at Falkenberg through a silence as ominous as the sky outside.

That didn't bother me as much as hearing Falkenberg dismiss the events in Georgia as trivial. My nightmares were still vivid down to the last image and scent. I wondered if the same dreams haunted Falkenberg. If he were not only trying to banish the Georgian Republic from the conversation but from his thoughts as well. In real terms, though, he was right. All the bloodshed had settled nothing. It had simply set the stage for a future I couldn't begin to predict.

Nordheim consulted his notes. "Some sixteen centuries ago," he began, slipping on his half-glasses to make his perusal official, "Georgian monks removed one hundred scrolls from the Library at Alexandria."

"Legend," Falkenberg said. "And that is being generous."

"History," Nordheim insisted. "Not of the textbook variety perhaps, but no less accurate. You traced the Scrolls to the monastery where they were taken and sent Mr. Doran to retrieve a digital copy."

"If any Scrolls were taken were taken from the library at Alexandria, it was during religious vandalism of the Serapaeum in A.D. 391. Construction of the monastery started in A.D. 737 and finished in A.D. 739. Your statement is a chronological impossibility."

Sometimes Falkenberg astonished me. He had been interested enough to ask the history of the monastery while I was busy giving myself up for dead. Nordheim was less impressed.

"I did not state, and did not mean to imply, that the Scrolls were taken directly to the monastery from Alexandria. They were, until a few weeks ago, housed there. Your Mr. Doran has established as much."

"Owen," Falkenberg said, "these good people have come at considerable expense and inconvenience. Please tell them everything you have established about the Alexandria Scrolls."

"I haven't established anything," I said. "An obscure librarian claimed to have stumbled on a legend that had Georgian monks pilfering Scrolls from the Library at Alexandria. Whether she actually found such a legend or was simply put up to saying she had by unscrupulous antiquities dealers, I have no way to know."

Beatte Czhed was an unlovely introvert who, like me and a lot of other people, was doomed to a life in the shadows. That, and her feelings for Eddington, would have made her an easy mark. A glance at Barbara, who had steered me to Beatte Czhed, produced no reaction. I was kidding myself if I thought I could get under her skin. I went back to my spiel.

"It does seem suspicious that her discovery coincided with an offer by the Georgian Orthodox Church to sell a number of scrolls written in Greek. Even more suspicious that a digital copy was handed over to a representative of the Falkenberg Foundation, one of the few private organizations positioned to arrange for the translation necessary to support a sale."

I had no doubt that Friar Bones has spotted me for a prize sucker, but the contents of the CD he foisted off on me had sunk the hook. Once I had seen the densely-packed old writing, I had to know what it said and what it meant.

"Until that translation is complete," I concluded, "we won't know what the Scrolls contain. Until their relics are dated, we won't know how old they are. I am aware of no forensic test that would establish whether they were ever housed at, or even passed through, the Library at Alexandria. That could well be puffery to inflate the price."

Truth be told, I believed absolutely in the provenance of the Scrolls. Saying otherwise, even to deflect a couple of pompous jerks, was hard to swallow. I wished I had something to wash it down with.

Falkenberg's doctors had forbidden him to drink and he had decided we all would be better off with clear heads.

"Mr. Doran's opinions are not necessarily those of the Foundation," he said, "but his summary of the evidence, or rather the lack of it, is complete as far as I know."

"So," Nordheim said, "you would like to be seen as innocent victims of some international flim-flam?"

"I wouldn't like that at all," Falkenberg said. "Although it may be the case."

"It is not," Nordheim shot back. "And when I have answers to the questions I have brought, I will have proof."

The preliminaries were over. Nordheim was ready to get down to business. The room fell silent, amplifying the rattle of rain on the windows. I felt perspiration under my collar.

In the two weeks since the events at Roche Harbor, Nordheim was the first law enforcement official I had seen. It had been two weeks of nervous waiting, not daring to contact anyone for fear I would draw attention to myself. Finally a cryptic e-mail from Falkenberg. I was to pack some business clothes and fly down for a conference.

Jerry was here when I arrived. He laid out what to say and what not to say while we ate our way through a shrimp creole that Sofia had whipped up for lunch. Falkenberg offered no insight into what had happened to him after we had been separated in Georgia, or how he felt about it. Jerry didn't like facing the authorities on short information, with no clue what was really on Falkenberg's mind. That might be the only thing he and I would ever agree on.

Chapter 31

Off-the-rack suits weren't cut for Nordheim's beanpole frame and when he stood his coat and trousers sagged in more places than they fit. The comic look was a schizophrenic contrast with the purposeful strides that brought him across the carpet to loom over Falkenberg.

"You were informed of the existence of the Alexandria Scrolls by Professor Roald Eddington, were you not?"

"I don't recall."

Nordheim turned on Barbara. "Did you or did you not introduce Professor Eddington to Mr. Falkenberg?"

"I did."

"And did Professor Eddington discuss the Alexandria Scrolls with Mr. Falkenberg?"

"Not in my presence."

"Professor Eddington kept you informed of those discussions," Nordheim insisted.

"Roald could be long-winded. I'm afraid I tuned out a great deal of what he said."

"Mrs. Wren, you are a dealer in black market antiquities. Any mention of the Alexandria Scrolls would have your attention. If you say otherwise, then you are a liar."

Barbara was unruffled.

Falkenberg was unhappy. "Inspector, this is my home. I will have my guests treated with respect."

Rosalinda Baca was uncompromising. "Mr. Falkenberg, would you like to submit to a court-ordered medical examination to determine your fitness for travel?"

Falkenberg subsided.

Nordheim's next stop was Mary Ann. "You are quoted as saying Professor Eddington was slain by a group called the Mighty Men. Is this correct?"

Mary Ann stared straight ahead. "I wish to assert my right to legal representation during any questioning."

Nordheim opened his mouth to speak but shut it when Rosalinda Baca cleared her throat. This was her party and she was not a woman to be trifled with.

"We acknowledge that you are entitled to counsel in regard to your arrest for investigation of criminal conspiracy," she assured Mary Ann. "This matter, however, involves activities outside U.S. jurisdiction. Inspector Nordheim merely wishes to know if you can clarify certain issues beyond the scope of your detention."

Mary Ann repeated herself. When she had been among religious zealots, she had adapted by parroting scripture. Now she was among jailbirds and she chanted their mantra. However resilient she might be, this couldn't be easy for her. Vestiges of Presbyterian guilt nagged at me. I had put her loopy rant on the public record and now I owed her some support.

"She was just repeating what she had been told," I said.

Nordheim turned on me. "You said an evangelist named Skinner blamed Eddington for the failure of his own efforts to have the Scrolls stolen from the monastery."

It was my turn in the barrel and I didn't have any answers. The Feds might or might not have Judson and his crew in custody. Their surveillance might have turned up any number of random facts and they might have spun any number of theories based on them. Anything I said might trap me in a spider web of law enforcement fantasies.

"I was speculating," I confessed.

"Based on what?" Nordheim demanded.

I described my conversation with Lew Manders, ending with, "I'm only guessing that Skinner hired him, that the monastery was his target and that it was the monks who ambushed his party."

"It has the ring of truth," Nordheim said with a grim smile. "Eastern churches have long been sanctuaries of last resort for men who would otherwise perish through the workings of law or revenge. Their price is banishment to isolated monasteries and absolute obedience to their word. The Scrolls were guarded by a particularly nasty bunch, including the former Deputy Commander of the Secret Police in the old Soviet Republic. He is seven feet tall and is said to have at least one murder against his soul for every inch of his height."

I was pretty sure Friar Bones amounted to more than just a cardboard villain from a cold war espionage movie. Men as tough and self-reliant as he was weren't in the habit of seeking refuge. If he joined a monastic order, it was for personal reasons. He didn't need defending to the likes of Interpol, so I kept my mouth shut.

Nordheim turned his attention back to Falkenberg. "What arrangements have you made with the Georgian Orthodox Church to sell the Scrolls?"

"None," Falkenberg said.

"We have affidavits from officers of the Georgian military that you were found with battle injuries in a forest near the monastery where the Scrolls were kept. Numerous dead and seriously injured Russian and Chechen nationals were found in the same area."

"What was that medical term again, Jerry? Traumatic memory dysfunction?"

Jerry piped up immediately, rattling away about Falkenberg's fragile psyche and the damage questioning could do to his emotional health. Nordheim paid no attention to the rant.

"Mr. Falkenberg, we are far from naïve. The Church can not simply place the Scrolls for sale on the black market without repercussions. What better way to conceal the transfer than a skirmish in which it appeared that the treasure was lost to Chechen bandits?"

"Do you know that it wasn't?" Falkenberg asked.

"We know very well what became of the Scrolls," Nordheim said. "Don't we, Ms. Talemantes?"

I was confused until Nordheim turned to Sofia.

She met his gaze directly, saying nothing and betraying nothing beyond contempt for law enforcement born and nurtured during her years as a slave in the sex industry.

Nordheim was no stranger to the look. "You are an associate of Faraz Al Nouri, also known as The Scalded Woman. A dealer in black market antiquities."

"I am acquainted with Mrs. Al Nouri."

"You accompanied her to Georgia."

"It is not seemly for a Muslim woman to travel alone."

"You were present when Georgian monks delivered the Scrolls to her."

"I saw no scrolls."

"They were sealed in aluminum containers."

"Then I could not have seen them."

"Eyewitnesses reported that you were armed, Ms. Talemantes. What were you protecting?"

"It was an isolated region. There were rumors of women travelers being molested."

"Ms. Talemantes, you were wearing body armor and carrying an assault rifle. Tallying ammunition and grenades, you had half again your body weight in military hardware."

"I am easily frightened."

"The Scrolls were loaded onto a cargo aircraft. You flew out of the country with them. You and the Scalded Woman."

"I saw no Scrolls."

"Where did the plane land?"

"I was not familiar with the place."

"But it was in Iran."

"If you know, why do you ask?"

"Where did the Scalded Woman take the Scrolls when they were unloaded?"

"Mrs. Al Nouri and I parted company. I heard my friend, Mr. Falkenberg, had been injured, so I came to America to be with him."

"Mr. Falkenberg, of course, knows full well where the Scrolls went."

Silence earned Falkenberg an extended glare.

"You knew," Nordhcim pressed on, "that the cargo was taken to a port on the Shatt Al Arab and loaded onto a freighter bound for America."

"I was indisposed at the time," Falkenberg reminded him.

"So you dispatched your toady, Mr. Doran, in your stead."

Falkenberg raised his eyebrows in mock surprise. "Owen, have I dispatched you?"

"Not recently," I said.

"You," Nordheim told Falkenberg, "instructed Mr. Doran to invite three women known to be under suspicion to dinner at a smuggler's haven called Roche Harbor."

Falkenberg shook his head at me. "Owen, what have I told you about abusing your position with the Foundation to go skirt chasing?"

I gave him a mousey smile.

Nordheim strode to where I sat. "This is not a joke. While you were distracting the authorities in the San Juan Islands, the Scrolls were landed quietly at Coos Bay, Oregon, and flown from the adjoining Newport airfield to an unknown destination."

"In the first place," I said, "I don't think the Roche Harbor Chamber of Commerce would appreciate your calling their tourist paradise a smugglers' haven. In the second, you can't seriously suggest that three ladies and I disrupted the entire border security apparatus of the most powerful nation in the world."

There was no doubt that my pathetic scheme had been co-opted as diversion by the Scalded Woman but her success required a certain level of ineptitude on the part of U.S. law enforcement. That wasn't an avenue Nordheim wanted to pursue.

"Mrs. Wren," he said, moderating his tone. "I fail to understand how a woman of your refinement could have involved herself in potentially violent activity."

Her smile conceded nothing.

"Had the pursuit helicopter been cleared to use its weapons systems," he said, "it is unlikely there would have been any survivors."

It was also unlikely they would have been cleared to fire. The risk of sending irreplaceable archaeological treasures to the bottom of Puget Sound was too great. Nordheim's frustration suggested the Scalded Woman's crew had abandoned the speedboat in Canada and made a clean getaway.

"Was it some test of nerve?" Nordheim asked. "Did Mrs. Al Nouri demand that you prove your courage before you would be allowed to participate in the sale of the Scrolls?"

That hadn't occurred to me. The Scalded Woman's scheme had called for considerable bravery from both Barbara and Sofia. It was clear that the Scalded Woman had eyes and ears inside Skinner's organization, but there was no guarantee that Skinner's people would follow the script. They could have improvised, or panicked, at any time. The whole thing could have erupted into an exchange of gunfire.

Barbara had passed her ordeal then, and she was unfazed by Nordheim's scrutiny now. He turned to Falkenberg.

"Sir, you are on intimate terms with two women involved in the sale of black market antiquities. If you have something that will distance you from them, something that will preserve your reputation and that of your foundation, this is the time to present it."

"Intimate is an overstatement. However I do value the friendship of both ladies and have no wish to distance myself from either."

Jerry took over. "As Mr. Falkenberg's counsel, allow me to summarize the legal points of the situation. All of your allegations require the existence of an entity you refer to as the Alexandria Scrolls. You cannot produce the Scrolls in a court of law. Nor can you establish their existence by good evidence. Your tale of tin boxes and secret flights proves nothing. Mr. Doran's digital media cannot be connected to physical artifacts. Offers by black market dealers to sell items they purport to be the Scrolls are meaningless. They are career criminals. Their representations are void of merit. Someday the provenance of the Alexandria Scrolls may be established by good science and diligent scholarship. Today the Scrolls are vapor. You have no case."

Rosalinda Baca stood, plowed across the room and fixed steely eyes on Falkenberg. "I will not tolerate mockery of the law. I am referring the entire matter to the FBI with a strong recommendation for full investigation of all aspects of your activities. I expect all of you to be under indictment by the end of this year and in prison by the end of next."

She marched out of the house.

Nordheim followed. There was no reason for him to stay. We were toast. And on a more practical level, she probably had the keys to the rental car. Mary Ann's escort handcuffed her and took her out.

Jerry let out a long sigh. "Well, Alex, it looks like we are in for a siege. I don't like to criticize but a more conciliatory attitude might have helped."

"On the contrary," Falkenberg said, "things could not have gone any better."

Jerry and the two women stared at him. I sank into the sanctuary of the gondola chair. Falkenberg had something in mind, and when he got ideas, trouble couldn't be far behind.

Chapter 32

"Poor Alex," Barbara said. She stood and went to Falkenberg's side and put a comforting hand on his forearm. "This must have been an ordeal. Do get some rest. I'll look in on you later in the week."

Sofia stood. "Alexander, you will be all right while I walk Barbara to her car?"

"You ladies take your time."

Sofia followed Barbara out and drew the pocket doors together behind them. The doors weighed a hundred pounds each. They moved with the touch of a finger and the silence of doom. Once they closed, no sound penetrated. Curiosity brought me to my feet. I went to the window where I could watch the two women descend the stairs to the drive.

"Owen," Falkenberg said to my back, "women exist for two purposes. Recreation and reproduction. Anything else is a trap for the unwary."

It would do no good to remind him that I had always been one of life's spectators, that people-watching was just amusement for me. To him, people were chess pieces, to be maneuvered wherever they best suited his purpose of the moment. I retreated into the depths of the room where the fruits of his scheming had installed a beautifully inlaid sideboard and set about mixing myself a drink.

Jerry tried to sound upbeat. "At least we have a last name on Alex's mystery woman. I can get a background."

Falkenberg dismissed the idea with a snort. "Women like Sofia can't afford the luxury of a name. Talemantes is just a few syllables on a graft-issue passport."

It was a reminder that Sofia lived in a world where her next breath might depend on how convincingly she could lie. I didn't want to believe she had lied to me. At the same time I didn't want to believe everything she had told me. I had a lot of feelings to sort out, none of which concerned anyone but me.

Jerry's concern was his backside. "Alex, that woman is part of an international conspiracy."

"We need her," Falkenberg said. "And we need her conspiracy."

Jerry stared in disbelief. "Alex, you're not thinking rationally." He shook his head. "This is my fault. I never should have allowed an interview while your doctor had you on Oxycontin."

Falkenberg didn't take kindly to being patronized. "Listen, you two, and listen carefully. I want to get something settled before Sofia gets back."

I returned to the window where I had good view of the driveway below. The two women stood beside a white Lexus coupe, coats drawn tight against the gusty wind, hoods up to protect them from the slanting rain, engrossed in conversation.

"It looks like we have a few minutes," I said, bracing myself with a stiff belt.

Falkenberg gave Jerry and me one hard look apiece. "We have a duty to shepherd the contents of the Alexandria Scrolls into the public domain."

Jerry sounded as confused as I felt. "Alex, you have the foremost classical scholars in the country working on translation."

"And as long as they are working on it," Falkenberg shot back, "the academic world will be hanging on their every revelation. As soon as they finish, they go back on the shelf with the rest of the fossils. It took decades to make the Dead Sea Scrolls public."

I was tired of Falkenberg's demands that everything be done in the next five minutes. "Okay, Alex, so they string the job out. Pad their moment of glory. The Scrolls have been rotting for sixteen centuries. What difference can another sixteen months make? Or even sixteen years?"

"How many Scrolls are there?" Falkenberg asked.

"Fifty seven."

"Not according to your so-called legend."

"I was suckered. The legend is a modern fiction."

"Ginned up by people who knew how many Scrolls exist today," Falkenberg said.

"And had any number of reasons to lie about the count," I pointed out.

"Think about it," Falkenberg ordered. "The monks who lifted the Scrolls from Alexandria knew they were at risk from fire, flood, theft, decay, you name it. They wouldn't store everything in one location."

"Why not split fifty-fifty?"

"They probably sent half the donkeys carrying the Scrolls to one location, half to another. Uneven loads left them with a fifty-seven, forty-three distribution."

"How much of that do you know for a fact?" I asked.

"Enough to risk my neck in Georgia."

"Our necks," I corrected.

Falkenberg gave me the contemptuous look he reserved for whiners. "The Georgian Orthodox Church has released fifty seven scrolls to see what price they'll bring before they put the other forty three up for sale. The highest price, therefore the best chance of surfacing the other scrolls, can be had on the black market. Collectors who buy on the black market won't pay top dollar for the Scrolls without knowing what they contain. That means immediate translation."

A gust of wind threw rain against the window and took me back to the stormy night I had handed the CD over to Falkenberg. I realized I had been suckered even then.

"You demanded exclusive rights to the Scrolls knowing you'd tweak my authority issues. You wanted me to shop the Scrolls on my own to turn translation into a horse-race."

"You could have been more aggressive," he said. "A no-name department head at a California backwater isn't much of a threat to the Ivy League crowd."

"You also sent me into Georgia as bait, to see how many of the Scrolls you could get your hands on."

"I didn't expect any recovery. I just needed a fresh set of eyes on the subject. A skeptic who didn't believe in anything. Not even himself. Someone who might give me an idea whether this was a con or the real deal."

I didn't know whether that was an endorsement or a criticism. I didn't have a comeback.

Jerry always had one. "Alex, you don't know these scrolls came from the Library at Alexandria. Owen said there was no evidence."

"There will be marking on the Scrolls, or something in the content, to establish source," Falkenberg said.

Jerry was taken aback by the confidence in his declaration. "How do you know? They haven't been thoroughly examined. Much less translated."

"The Georgian Orthodox Church knows what's in them. They wouldn't tout them as coming from the Library at Alexandria unless they were certain proof would emerge. There is too much money at stake."

"If the Church gets enough from the fifty seven scrolls," Jerry warned, "they won't need to sell the others."

"The ten-forty mafia isn't going away," Falkenberg said. "The Georgian Orthodox Church will need money as long as they are under siege by Evangelicals. The trick is to get them to sell the remaining Scrolls before they start in on the silly-ass icons and other baubles."

Jerry was running out of arguments and tension infiltrated his voice. "Alex, you're talking about conspiracy to traffic in prohibited antiquities."

"Not all history is dug out of the ground. A manuscript from Archimedes turned up in another monastery. Some well-meaning monk had scraped the page clean to make a prayer book and now technicians are trying to raise the original writing with X-rays. Priceless history is at risk of damage and decay. We have an obligation to recover and preserve it by any means necessary."

"That could put the Foundation in grave danger," Jerry protested. "It could imperil everything we've worked to build."

"The Foundation was organized to delve into history. History doesn't exist to support the foundation."

The Foundation was all Jerry had going for him. Without it he was just another lawyer trying to hustle up litigation. And I was just another bean counter.

"What's in the other forty three Scrolls," I asked Falkenberg.

"Only the Georgian Orthodox Church knows that."

"So you're just guessing at their value."

"Use your head. Any sensible person testing the market would dangle the smaller piece. The only reason to deviate from that logic is if the smaller piece is worth more than the larger. Even after the fifty seven are translated, we still won't know half of what the Alexandria Scrolls have to reveal."

I didn't have a reasonable argument so I stared out the window and sipped morosely at my drink.

"How are we doing?" Falkenberg asked.

"Two chicks on one cell phone. They'll be at it for a while."

"I should have asked how you are doing."

"Terrific," I said. "I've finished my course of medication for staph infection. The last hole has almost closed. The nightmares should start receding soon. Of course, I just found out that I've been suckered again but that happens all the time."

"What were you expecting?" Falkenberg demanded. "A Hollywood ending? Pot of gold at the end of the rainbow? Suck face with a spunky young heroine? Ride off into the sunset?"

It seemed like a century since I had thought in those terms. I knew better now. No footnote in history for poor Owen. Just the usual thankless work behind the scenes. And a duty I knew I couldn't shirk. The world was entitled to know what was in the Scrolls, regardless of cost or peril.

As far as spunky young heroines were concerned, they wouldn't last two seconds in this game. The chicks at this level had smarts, experience and steel nerves. Greed was their creed and God help anyone who got in their way. But somewhere along the line they had become real people and I couldn't help being fascinated by both of them. I glanced out the window.

Barbara put the cell phone into her purse and climbed into her Lexus. Smooth acceleration took her down the driveway and out of sight. She appeared briefly on the Coast Highway, making speed. Sofia started up toward the house. I turned back to Falkenberg.

"Time's up," I said.

"This is not limited to the Alexandria Scrolls," he said. "If we succeed, we establish a business model that can be used to extract writings from other sanctuaries. If we fail, no end of history could be left to rot away."

I knew now why he had hosted today's party. He wanted publicity, and there was nothing like a Federal investigation wrapped in rumors of international intrigue to generate the odd headline. There were two audiences. Knowing their coup could be snatched away at any second would keep pressure on the translators. And anyone else with old writings to sell would become aware of a lucrative outlet. Falkenberg was ready to paint targets on all of our backs to make that happen.

He used the motor controls to turn his wheelchair to confront Jerry. To Falkenberg, everything was an instrument of intimidation. He was learning how to manipulate this one.

"In or out?" he demanded.

Jerry was forced to decide between the law he was sworn to uphold and the law he was desperate to practice.

"Well, of course, as your attorney, Alex, I'm always there for you."

Tactics trumped ethics. I could practically hear the cheers from the Bar Association.

"Owen?" Falkenberg demanded.

Falkenberg had gambled his life in Georgia. He fought at the monastery. He went with Gregoriev to break the Chechen encirclement. The skirmish left him in agony in a desolate forest not knowing whether he would live or die. This was no whim for him. It was the quest of a lifetime. Maybe I had caught the fever from him, or maybe I was just intoxicated with my own dreams.

"You know I'm in," I said. "You knew it before you asked."

The pocket doors slid open and Sofia floated into the living room, all smiles and fragrance. The game had begun in earnest. With Falkenberg facing a long recuperation I knew a lot of it would fall on my shoulders.

* * * END * * *

83685011R00104

Made in the USA
San Bernardino, CA
29 July 2018